"Kiss Me Back," Jordan Murmured.

When she shook her head, he smiled against her mouth. "Fine. Don't kiss me back." He nipped at her jaw, trailed kisses down her neck. "I'll just enjoy this for both of us."

She was crumbling fast. Breaking down into tiny little pieces of need. When his mouth covered hers again and his tongue swept over her bottom lip, she shuddered. She hated that he had this power over her, that he could make her feel things she didn't want to feel. Flattening her palms on his chest, she pushed. "Stop."

For a long moment, he didn't move, then slowly he dropped his hands from her arms and stepped back. "You're my wife, Alexis."

"*Was* your wife," she said, shaking her head. "I filed the annulment papers. Just because you didn't sign them doesn't change a thing."

"Like hell it doesn't." Irritation sharply edged his words and his voice rose. "Right or wrong, like it or not, you're still my wife."

Dear Reader,

When I begin the process of writing a book, some characters hold back and make me work hard to unravel their secrets. Others are in my face and extremely vocal, quite eager for me to hear their side of the story and make sure I get it right.

Jordan and Alexis definitely fit into the latter description.

Both are stubborn, both equally determined—not only to deny the passion simmering between them, but to hide a safely guarded secret that is better left in the past.

Alas, Jordan and Alexis never should have told me their secret. Because you know what they say, dear reader, "I can keep a secret, it's the people I tell who can't...."

Mum's the word,

Barbara McCauley

P.S. Be sure to visit my Web site for more secrets: www.BarbaraMcCauley.com.

BARBARA McCAULEY

BLACKHAWK'S AFFAIR

™ Silhouette®

Desire

Published by Silhouette Books

America's Publisher of Contemporary Romance

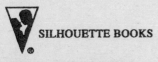

SILHOUETTE BOOKS

ISBN-13: 978-0-373-76790-8
ISBN-10:   0-373-76790-0

BLACKHAWK'S AFFAIR

Books in Barbara McCauley's SECRETS! series

Silhouette Desire

Silhouette Romantic Suspense

Silhouette Books

Summer Gold
"A Wolf River Summer"

Blackhawk Legacy

BARBARA McCAULEY,

who has written more than thirty novels for Silhouette Books, lives in Southern California with her own handsome hero husband, Frank, who makes it easy to believe in and write about the magic of romance. Barbara's stories have won and been nominated for numerous awards, including the prestigious RITA® Award from the Romance Writers of America, Best Desire of the Year from *Romantic Times BOOKreviews* and Best Short Contemporary from the National Readers' Choice Awards.

This book is dedicated to Michelle Thorne,
a Warrior Goddess with a heart of gold.
You inspire me, dear friend!

One

Jordan Alastair Grant had built an empire keeping one step ahead of the competition and two steps ahead of his past. He'd been rich, he'd been poor, he'd been rich again. Money itself meant little to him. The exclusive cars, the custom built houses, the private company jet— as far as he was concerned, they were all just props. A means to an end. It was winning that truly made his blood rush. That sharp kick of pleasure deep in his gut when an opponent either threw in the towel or went down for the count.

Business was just a game, he'd always thought. Stocks, oil, investments—each transaction, every endeavor, just another roll of the dice, one more playing piece on the board.

He had the look of power. Six-foot-four, precision-cut, thick, dark hair, the solid, muscled body of an athlete he kept well-toned with daily workouts into his gym. His face, roughly chiseled and hard-edged, had the ability to intimidate with one razor-sharp glance from his bottle-green eyes, or charm with a simple tilt of his firm, wide mouth. His dark slash of brows, depending on his mood, or his need, could cut an adversary at his knees or make a woman swoon.

And if some people might think he was cold and calculating, what did it matter to him? As long as he got what he wanted, he didn't much give a damn what anyone thought.

He heard the landing gear lower on the jet and glanced at his Rolex. Right on schedule.

"We'll be landing in ten minutes, Mr. Grant."

Denise, the stewardess, moved toward him from the galley. An attractive redhead with a dimpled, beauty pageant smile and hazel eyes, she was a temporary replacement for Jordan's permanent flight staff.

The past few years he'd traveled more often than he liked, but with offices in Dallas, Lubbock and Houston, not to mention the West Coast affiliate, there hadn't been much choice. At thirty-four, he'd had enough of the daily grind of twelve hour days, seven days a week, most of it spent in board meetings or on a plane. Jordan had put the hours and sweat into his companies and other ventures, made his fortune. He'd enjoyed the challenge of it all when he was younger, but he was ready to move on now—or to be more accurate, he was ready to go back.

Back to his roots.

Jordan had been raised on Five Corners—twenty thousand acres of prime East Texas land that included cattle, lumber and oil. Richard Grant, Jordan's father, had been a genteel, socialite Bostonian with connections, but no money. Enter Kitty Turner, Jordan's mother, the daughter of a wealthy rancher with truckloads of money, but no connections.

It was a match—merger—made in heaven.

But while Richard may have appreciated and enjoyed the money that came with his marriage to Kitty, he detested everything about ranching and living in East Texas. The isolation, the physical labor, the camaraderie of the "good old boys." Richard had considered Five Corners beneath him.

Lost in his thoughts, Jordan hadn't realized Denise was still standing beside him, asking him something. He glanced up at the flight attendant, realized she'd asked him if he'd like more coffee.

"Thank you, no."

She leaned over him to collect his empty cup. "Shall I have the pilot notify your driver?"

"Not necessary." The subtle brush of the woman's hand across his arm did not go unnoticed—or the lingering eye contact. "I have a friend picking me up."

"Is there anything else I can do for you, sir?"

He shook his head, watched her turn and slowly saunter away to prepare for landing. He was certain the woman could do many things, but today, he only had one woman on his mind.

One with raven hair, sapphire eyes, endless legs.

He still remembered the feel of those legs wrapped around his waist.

He shrugged off the memory, and the pinch

to his pride when those legs had walked out on him. Okay, so maybe it was more than a pinch, he admitted reluctantly. Maybe it was more like the swing of a wrecking ball straight to his gut.

But that was eight years ago. He thought he'd been in love. Worse, he'd thought she'd been in love. It was a mistake he hadn't repeated.

The wheels of the small jet touched down smoothly on the small, private air strip, bumped a bit, then taxied to a stop at the end of the asphalt runway. He glanced out the window, saw the familiar green of the surrounding East Texas forest, ablaze now with fall colors. He'd grown up in those woods, played army and built forts there when he was a boy, broke his arm jumping off a rock into the lake when he was fourteen, and when he was sixteen, crashed his first truck—a brand-new, V-8, 486 silver Ford with black leather interior—straight into a hickory pine. He still had the thin, jagged scar over his left eyebrow where he'd hit the steering wheel with his forehead.

Jordan stared deeper into the thick trees, thought of other experiences in those woods, experiences of a more intense, sexual nature. Memories that would make a schoolgirl blush

She wouldn't like him being here, he knew,

but it didn't matter. After eight years, it was just too damn bad what she liked or didn't like.

It was time.

October had always been Alexis Blackhawk's favorite time of year. When the cloying heat of humid summer days began to soften, the nights turned long and cool, the air crisp. As a child, she'd loved the soft yellows of the cottonwoods, the earthy russets of oak, the vibrant orange of roadside pumpkin stands.

At the moment, however, what she especially loved was the shiny red convertible she'd just shifted into fourth gear. With the open road ahead of her, Mary J. Blige on the radio and the whip of the night wind through her brand-new, chic-salon, chin-length haircut, Alexis couldn't help but think, *Life is good.*

She took the turn off the highway a smidgen too fast, held tight to the wheel as the car skidded sideways. Smiling, she flattened the sole of her Jimmy Choo high heel against the accelerator, spitting dust and gravel off the car's rear tires as she raced down the familiar dirt road leading to Stone Ridge Stables. In spite of the bumps and dips, the sports car handled like a dream, and the power of the engine hummed in her head and sang in her blood. *I just might have to buy me one of these when I get home,* she thought, though living in New York, it would be frivolous, especially since she wouldn't have much opportunity to drive it, anyway.

Still, she could certainly afford to be frivolous, she knew, and her smile widened. Inheriting millions from a grandfather she'd never known had given her the ability—and the freedom—to be as absurdly frivolous as she wanted. Overnight, she'd gone from two maxed out credit cards, an overdrawn checking account and less than two weeks away from having her electricity turned off, to having more money than she knew what to do with.

Not that she hadn't figured it out quickly, of course. After a three day clothes shopping marathon on Fifth Avenue, she'd found and bought the apartment of her dreams on the West Side. It was as perfect as perfect gets. After she moved in, she intended to do her part to support the Gross National Product by tastefully furnishing every big, beautiful, high-ceilinged room, not to mention filling the walk-in closet in her master suite.

So many shoes, she thought, so little time.

Her headlights flashed across a pasture where sleepy cows barely lifted their heads to acknowledge their midnight visitor. At the edge of the stables, she flipped off the radio, then cut the lights as she rolled to a stop in front of the house where she'd been born.

She hadn't been home for a while—over a year—but nothing had changed. For that matter, nothing had changed on her family's ranch in her entire twenty-seven years. Same clapboard white, same black antebellum shutters, same honeysuckle climbing voraciously up the two-story porch columns. She breathed in the scent of it, felt the stillness, heard the nightsong of a mockingbird and the deep croak of a bullfrog.

There were memories here. Some she took comfort in. Others she preferred to forget.

She cut the engine and stepped out of the car, stared at the dark house while she rolled her tired shoulders. Since her sisters and brother weren't expecting her until tomorrow afternoon, they would all be asleep. The excitement of living on a ranch, she thought, shaking her head and smiling. She wasn't sure which was worse—going to bed before 1:00 a.m., or getting up at six.

With a sigh, she left her suitcases in the trunk, then grabbed her overnight bag from the front seat and crept into the house. Living in the city for the past nine years, she'd almost forgotten the blackness of a night without a moon. When her heels clicked on hardwood entry, she slipped her shoes off and felt her way across the floor, remembered her days as a teenager, sneaking in past her curfew, praying that Big Brother Trey wouldn't hear her.

He always did, of course, and their ensuing argument would not only wake the rest of the house, but the bunkhouse and next county, as well. She'd tell him to stop treating her like a baby, he'd tell her to stop acting like one. She'd tell him she didn't have to do what he said, he'd tell her until someone bigger and meaner came along, yes she did.

Since there weren't too many men in Stone Ridge bigger than Trey—and in her opinion, no one meaner—he'd always win. Kiera and Alaina would always sympathize with her, behind closed doors, but they never interceded or questioned Trey's authority. He was the man of the house, the one who had stepped up and taken charge after their father had left.

And her mother, Alexis remembered those days with a flash of sadness, her mother simply hadn't the ability to deal with an unruly teenager. Most days her mother could barely make it out of bed, let alone run a ranch or be a parent. So Trey had done it all, taken on all the responsibilities, ran the family with the same iron fist he ran the ranch. Not once could she remember hearing him complain.

There were things Alexis was sorry for, things she'd said, things she'd done to make her brother's life more difficult. But the past was the past, she knew, and regret was a useless emotion. She'd managed to get grants and work enough side jobs so she could go to college, had gotten her degree in fashion, and somewhere along the way, she'd like to think that she'd grown up. She had a dream job as an editor with *Impression* magazine, a terrific man she'd just started dating and now, all that money. Every day when she woke up, she had to pinch herself.

The fact that Kiera and Alaina were both suddenly in love with terrific men, and both engaged, was icing on the cake—the wedding cake, she thought with a smile.

Kiera's wedding was less than a week away, Alaina's following closely behind. They'd all planned this time together at the ranch as a last hurrah—a chance to reconnect before husbands and babies took over their lives.

Everything would be different now, of course, Alexis thought with a mixture of sadness and pleasure. But still, it was good, all good, and she knew it wouldn't be long before the sound of tiny feet would be pattering across these glossy hardwood floors. She decided she'd make one hell of an aunt.

Stubbing her toe on the leg of an entry table, Alexis bit back the curse, waited for the pain to subside, then slowly made her way to the stairs. She knew exactly where to step to avoid all the creaks, a little trick she'd learned in high school. At the top of the stairs, she felt her way to the guest bedroom, stepped inside and flipped on the light.

The bed and the surrounding floor were covered with cardboard boxes, some marked *Alaina*, some *Kiera*, and Alexis knew she wouldn't be sleeping in here tonight. With a sigh, she flipped off the light again, made her way across the hall, then slipped into Alaina's bedroom. Though she couldn't see a thing in the darkness, Alexis heard the sound of Alaina's steady breathing and she crept toward the big, four poster bed. The mattress dipped when she sat on the edge, but Alaina didn't stir. Quietly, Alexis pulled off her beige blazer and crepe slacks, left her camisole on, then slid under the cool, crisp sheets.

If only for a few days, it felt good to be home.

Growing up, she and Alaina had shared a bedroom, laid awake many a night talking about boys and school, or complaining about Trey. If there was anything they had agreed on—Kiera included—it was that their big brother was a heartless bully.

A heartless bully they loved beyond life itself.

She thought of another man, one whom she'd also thought was a heartless bully, one whom she'd also loved deeply. But thoughts of that man only brought hurt, so she pushed him out of her mind. This was no time for shattered dreams, Alexis chastised herself. This was a time to celebrate, to be happy.

She laid on her side and snuggled under the sheets, stared into the darkness, until she finally gave in to the exhaustion of a long, busy day of work and travel. Closing her eyes, she slowly drifted off to sleep, with the strangest feeling that somewhere, something wasn't quite right....

* * *

There was a woman in his bed.

Jordan blinked a few times, just to make sure he wasn't still dreaming, then rubbed the sleep from his eyes.

Nope. No dream. There really *was* a woman in the bed next to him.

Hell of a way to wake up.

Her back was turned to him, and she hugged her pillow and the edge of the bed. He raised up on his elbow and in the pale gray of the early morning light, studied the outline of her long, slender body stretched out beside him. The ends of her thick, dark hair skimmed her graceful neck, and the lacy edge of a white camisole peeked out from under the sheets. Jordan lifted the sheet and lowered his gaze.

After all, someone had set a present in front of him, the least he could do was look at it.

White thong, he noted, and sucked in a breath through gritted teeth. Nice—make that *very* nice—rear end. On her hip, a small unicorn reared, its white mane flowing. She stirred, rolled to her back.

Well, well, well. Jordan raised a brow. His present just kept getting better.

She'd cut her hair, he noted, and decided that the shorter, tousled look fit her heart-shaped face extremely well. Though it was subtle, the angles of her high cheekbones had sharpened, as had the delicate line of her jaw. Her mouth hadn't changed, though. It was still just as wide and lush, tipped up at the corners. Still just as tempting.

She sighed softly, lifted one hand to rest beside her head. Her long fingers curled toward her smooth palm, her nails were perfectly manicured with pretty white, French tips. Remembering the feel of those hands on his skin, his pulse jumped.

If he was a gentleman, he supposed he could slip out of bed, at least pull on a pair of jeans before she woke up. He supposed he might even be able to leave the room without disturbing her, save her a bucket load of embarrassment when she opened her eyes and realized it wasn't her sister she'd crawled into bed with during the night.

But he wasn't feeling very gentlemanly at the moment, and besides—he settled his head into the palm of his hand and stared down at her— it wouldn't be nearly as much fun.

She smelled as good as she looked, he thought. Like a warm breeze on an exotic beach. He breathed the scent in, let his gaze travel down the slender column of her graceful neck, watched the peaceful rise and fall of her full breasts. This time, his pulse didn't just jump, it sprinted.

He slid a fingertip along her jaw and whispered her name. "Alexis."

When she didn't respond, he threw caution to the wind—hell, he was only human—and he let his finger glide smoothly down her neck, over the pulse at the base of her throat, her collarbone. Her skin was warm and soft as rose petals.

"Alexis."

He moved lower, skimmed his fingertips over the swell of her breast, watched her nipple harden under the thin cotton camisole. Lust shot like an arrow straight to his groin and he felt himself harden. Damn, but she tempted him, and his palm ached to cup her in his hand, his mouth ached to taste her.

He might have, but when her eyelashes, thick and dark against her smooth, golden skin, fluttered softly, he reluctantly reconsidered. She stirred, stretched one arm over her head as she drew in a deep breath, then sighed. When her lids slitted open, her sleepy, ocean-blue gaze met his.

"Mornin'," he murmured.

"Morning," she breathed and closed her eyes again.

He waited a beat, then two.

Her eyes flew open, focused now.

She squeaked at the same time she pushed away from him, her long legs caught in the sheets and she flopped over the edge of the mattress onto the floor.

Two

Please, please, *please* let this be a nightmare, Alexis thought frantically and squeezed her eyes shut. *Just let me wake up now, still in bed, my sister sleeping beside me....*

But based on the cold, hardwood floor pressing against her backside, the sting of pain vibrating up her elbow, and the lingering burn of his fingertip on her jaw, she had the horrible, awful feeling that she was, in fact, very much awake.

Which didn't make it any less of a nightmare.

She opened her eyes, groaned when she saw

him staring down at her, his gaze wickedly amused.

The urge to scramble away from him over- whelmed her, but with her legs still wrapped up in the sheets, she couldn't move, and realized if she tried, she'd pull loose the last little bit of sheet covering Jordan from the waist down.

"Was it something I said?" he asked, raising one brow.

She watched his gaze slide from her face down to her breasts, and she snagged a pillow from the bed, hugged it close. "What are you doing here?"

"Sleeping." He scrubbed a hand over his morning beard, then raked his fingers through his hair. "At least I was, until your snoring woke me up. You should see a doctor about that."

"I do not—" She stopped, frowned darkly. He'd always been able to ruffle her feathers, dammit. "You know perfectly well what I mean. What are you doing in Alaina's bed?"

"Come back up here with me—" he patted the bed beside him "—and I'll tell you."

"I most certainly will not." Struggling not to yell, she glanced at the bedside clock— 5:30 a.m.—prayed no one else in the house was up yet. Even if she was an adult, even if nothing had happened—or was *going* to happen—in this bedroom, the mere thought of Trey walking into the room and seeing her with Jordan like this made Alexis's stomach clench.

"Okay, be that way." He sighed, shook his head. "I'll come down there with you, then."

When he moved toward the edge of the four poster bed, her breath caught. She grabbed one of her high heels and pointed it at him. "Jordan Grant, don't you dare."

"You used to say that to me when you wanted me to kiss you."

She opened her mouth to deny it, but because she couldn't, frustration took over and she tossed the shoe at his head instead. Unfortunately, he managed to duck the missile, which sailed across the bed and landed with a thud against the wall.

Stupid, stupid. Biting her lip, Alexis held her breath, listened several seconds for the sound of footsteps from the hall outside. When she heard nothing, she slowly exhaled.

"Dammit, Jordan—" she whispered sharply "—what are you doing here?"

"Trey invited me."

"We agreed you wouldn't come to the ranch at the same time I was here." She tensed at the sound of water running through the pipes, knew that someone was up in the house, and it was most likely Trey.

"We never agreed on anything, sweetheart," Jordan said. "Which, I seem to recall, is the reason you walked out on me."

She wouldn't let him bait her into an argument, Alexis told herself. Especially not right now.

"I didn't *walk* out on you, *sweetheart*," she said, tilting her chin up. "I ran."

"Ouch." Wincing, he rubbed at his chest. "Touché, Allie."

Her satisfaction at wounding him was short-lived when her eyes followed the path of his hand. It was impossible not to notice that his broad chest was even broader and more muscled, more cut, than it had been eight years ago. It was also impossible not to remember what those hard muscles had felt like rippling under her fingers.

Instinctively she scooted back, and the sheet slid farther down his lean waist, revealing an arrow of dark masculine hair. Her pulse did a pole vault and she gasped, snapped her gaze up.

"You're in my sister's bed, naked?"

"Jealous?"

She refrained—barely—from hurling herself at him. She was going to kill him. Quietly, so Trey wouldn't hear. All she had to figure out was how to get his six-foot-four, two-hundred-twenty-pound body down the stairs and out of the house without anyone seeing. "Jordan, so help me—"

"You always were high-strung," he said, shaking his head. "But if it makes you feel any better, your sister isn't even here. Neither one of them are, for that matter. You're the only female in the house."

"What do you mean, my sisters aren't here?" She blew a thick strand of hair from her eyes, decided to let the high-strung comment go for the moment. "Where are they?"

"Don't know exactly." He yawned, scratched at his neck. "But Trey said something about them spending an extra day shopping in Houston since you weren't coming in until today."

They were shopping? Without her? They could have at least called, Alexis thought, mildly miffed she'd been left out, then froze when she heard bootsteps in the hall and realized she had a much bigger problem at the moment.

The steps stopped outside the bedroom door. She had visions of her brother walking in, his eyes narrowing at the sight of her sitting on the floor, half-naked, and Jordan in the bed, naked as the day he was born. Afraid to move, afraid to breathe, she stared at the door handle, waited for it to turn....

When the bootsteps moved away and she heard the familiar creak on the stairs, relief flooded through her. She closed her eyes and exhaled.

"Just like old times," Jordan said.

"No, it is not." She opened her eyes and clenched her teeth. "I'm not nineteen and impulsive, or so easily impressed by a handsome face and broad chest. I look for a little more depth in a relationship now, qualities beyond the physical."

"So I take it the sex hasn't been so good since we were together."

"I didn't say—" She caught herself, annoyed that he'd nearly sucked her right back into his little game of macho superiority. "My sex life, my *life*, for that matter, is none of your business. Now if you wouldn't mind turning around so I can get dressed and get out of here before Trey sees my car..."

He made no move to turn away or even avert his gaze. "You never used to be shy, Allie."

"You never used to be such a lech," she tossed back.

"If appreciating a beautiful woman's body makes me a lech, then fine, guilty as charged."

With a sigh, he rolled over, dragging the sheets with him and leaving Alexis without any covers. She scrambled for the slacks she'd pulled off before getting into bed and shimmied into them, but didn't bother with the blazer. All she wanted was to get out of this room, and hopefully sneak into Kiera's old bedroom before Trey realized that she'd come home last night. Even eight years ago, her brother hadn't known about her whirlwind relationship with his best friend—nor had anyone else, for that matter. She certainly didn't want them finding out now.

As far as she was concerned, she and Jordan never happened.

She stuffed her blazer and high heel into her bag, collected her shoe's mate, then hurried for the door and quietly turned the knob.

"Hey, Allie."

Frowning, she glanced over her shoulder, saw him lying on his back, arms behind his head. She cursed at the little jump in her pulse at the sight of him in the bed, shot him an impatient look.

"Nice tattoo."

She nearly choked on the swear word she had to swallow back, somehow managed to gently close the door—rather than slam it the way she really wanted to—and crept across the hall into her sister's bedroom.

Inside, she ran for the bed, dropped her face into a pillow and screamed.

The smell of coffee, bacon and pancakes finally enticed Alexis out of the bedroom. She hadn't been able to sleep after her early morning encounter with Jordan, anyway, and since she had no intention of hiding out from the man in her own brother's house, she'd decided she might as well face the dragon head on. She'd showered, pulled on the only change of clothes in her overnight bag—a simple indigo, V-neck sweater and a pair of Blue Snake jeans, then, out of habit, swiped on a dab of mascara. If she'd fussed with her hair a few moments longer than necessary, it was only because the cut was new and she hadn't gotten used to it yet.

Her primping had nothing to do with Jordan,

she told herself when she hit the bottom stair. Absolutely nothing at all.

He'd never actually told her why he was here, though she assumed it was because of the wedding, though now that she thought about it, Jordan had an office in Dallas, which was much closer to Wolf River than Stone Ridge. He had no reason to be here, staying at the ranch, though he'd said Trey had invited him, which still didn't make any sense.

She'd known that sooner or later their paths would cross, and she'd carefully orchestrated her life to make it later. Eight years' worth of later. She'd expected he'd be at Kiera's wedding, had even prepared herself for it. It obviously would have been easier to see him with a hundred other people around—much easier than waking up and finding him in bed with her.

But she was calm now, composed.

Dressed.

She heard the sound of male voices, the scrape of a chair across the wooden floor, the clatter of plates and silverware. Familiar sounds. The kitchen had always been the heart of this house, the one place the family had gathered, where they'd laughed, where they'd cried, where they'd screamed at each other. Where they'd comforted.

The first time she'd met Jordan had been in this kitchen. He'd been seventeen, she'd been ten, hiding from a manic mother determined to crush her rebellious daughter's wild ways. Under cross examination, Jordan hadn't given her up, even though he'd watched her duck behind the door in the mud room. She'd had a crush on him from that moment on—out of gratitude, she realized now. Misplaced appreciation for a simple gesture of compassion. It had taken her nine years to get his attention.

She'd spent the last eight years wishing she hadn't.

Squaring her shoulders, she breezed into the kitchen, forced a smile when Jordan and Trey both glanced up at her over their coffee cups.

"Mornin'." She moved toward her brother and kissed his cheek. "You need a shave, cowboy."

"You need some meat on your bones. Cookie—" Trey looked at the gray-haired man who'd been keeping their house and preparing their meals for more than twenty-five years "—give my sister a tall stack with extra butter."

"Just coffee for me, thanks." She smoothed a hand over the braid Cookie wore halfway down his back and gave him a peck on his weathered cheek. He grumbled that she was too skinny and she needed to eat, but the man was usually grumbling about something.

"I'll eat something later," she promised and glanced at Jordan. "My stomach's been off since I woke up. Hey, Jordan."

"Hey, Allie." Jordan nodded. "Long time no see."

"Well, you know what they say about time." Alexis took the mug of steaming coffee Cookie poured for her and leaned back against the white tiled kitchen counter. The amusement she'd seen in his green eyes earlier was gone. Now, she saw only the hard-edged businessman who commanded a room just by walking into it. Even in worn jeans and a denim shirt, Jordan Grant was a man who radiated power.

"It flies when you're having fun?" Jordan replied.

She lifted her cup and sipped. "That a long time is determined by which side of the bathroom door you're on."

"Some things never change." Shaking his

head, Trey plucked another pancake from a platter on the table. "I never understood why you two were always at each other's throats."

The expression stirred an image in Alexis's mind—of Jordan's mouth on her throat, her mouth on his. When his gaze met hers, she knew he was thinking exactly the same thing. Her cheeks warmed and she quickly looked away.

When she was younger, she had intentionally picked at Jordan or started fights so no one would know her true feelings. But that first summer she'd come home from college, the first time Jordan had looked at her like a woman and not a child, everything had changed between them. Everything except the fact that she still hadn't wanted Trey to know how she felt about his best friend, was certain that if he, or anyone, found out, it would end in disaster.

As it turned out, her and Jordan's relationship had ended in disaster without the help of anyone but themselves.

"Trey told me he was picking you up at the airport this afternoon," Jordan said conversationally.

She knew he was trying to unnerve her. Dammit if it wasn't working.

She speared a glance at him. "I caught a late flight last night and rented a car at the airport. I was hoping to surprise my family."

"Nothing you do surprises us, sis." Trey forked up a bite of pancake smothered in syrup. "But I would have moved the boxes off your bed if I'd known. Where'd you sleep?"

"I'm in Kiera's room," she said, which was true for the moment, but hadn't really answered the question of where she'd slept. "If I'd realized you had company, I wouldn't have come in early."

"Jordan's not company, and you know it." Trey washed the last of his pancake down with a swallow of coffee, then scraped his chair back from the table and stood. "I don't know what the feud is between you two, but I don't have the time or the inclination to referee. Why don't you both just kiss and make up and be done with it?"

"All right," Jordan said, offered his cheek.

Alexis frowned at him, was thankful when the phone rang and distracted the conversation. Cookie answered it, then signaled it was for him and limped out of the room. Her frown darkened and she looked back at her brother. "What's wrong with Cookie's leg?"

"Needs a hip replacement." Trey plucked his hat off a hook beside the back door. "Surgery's scheduled for next month."

She furrowed her brow. "What's he doing in here, standing on his feet?"

"Stubborn fool won't listen to me," Trey said. "Maybe you and your sisters can talk some sense into him."

Her history with stubborn men wasn't the best, Alexis thought, glancing at Jordan and Trey, but she'd do what she could. Cookie was more family than hired help, and she couldn't stand the thought of him being in pain. He'd been there with them through the darkest times, made them soup when they were sick, cocoa when it was cold and rainy. Baked their birthday cakes and holiday dinners. He'd always been here, she'd never considered there would be a time when he wouldn't be. Couldn't imagine the ranch without him.

"I'll be in the stables." Trey settled his hat on his head and looked at Jordan. "You might want to take a look at a few of my mares, since you're in the market again. We're going to auction in a couple of weeks, but I'll give you first pick."

Jordan nodded. "I'll be out shortly."

Alexis waited for Trey to leave, then narrowed a look at Jordan. "What does he mean, you're in the market again?"

"I'm moving back to Five Corners."

"What do you mean, you're moving back?" Coffee sloshed over the sides of her cup. "Your parents sold Five Corners seven years ago, right after their divorce."

"True." Jordan finished off the slice of bacon he'd picked up, then pushed his plate away. "They sold it to me."

"They what?" She stared at him, mouth open, eyes wide, didn't even try to hide the shock of his announcement.

"I was sick of their arguing over who got what and how much." He moved a shoulder. "I had my trust fund, so I bought it myself and until last month leased it out through one of my corporations."

Alexis felt as if her head was going to explode. Why didn't she know this? Why hadn't Trey ever mentioned that Jordan had bought Five Corners? Between her sisters not being here, Cookie's surgery and Jordan staying at the ranch, Alexis was beginning to feel as if no one bothered to tell her anything.

"Does that bother you, Allie?" Jordan asked quietly. "Me moving back to Stone Ridge?"

Did it bother her? Hell, yes. But she'd be damned if she'd let him know just how much. She wrapped her hands tightly around her coffee cup so he wouldn't see them shake and shrugged. "Just surprises me, that's all. West Texas property is much more popular with rich oil barons."

"True enough. But I'm not here for oil."

"Why are you here?"

He leaned back in his chair, leveled his gaze with hers. "I'm here for you."

Three

For the next three hours, Alexis fumed.

For you.

From her upstairs bedroom, she stared down at Jordan, who leaned against the corral fence, his long, sinewy arms draped over a metal rail while he watched one of the hands working with a big roan. She remembered all the times she'd stood in this very spot and secretly watched Jordan, all those years she'd pined for her brother's best friend and he hadn't given her a second glance.

For you.

He'd only said that to rattle her cage, she knew, and the fact that he'd succeeded annoyed her more than the comment itself. That, and Cookie walking back into the kitchen before she'd been able to respond.

Before Jordan had gone out the back door and headed for the corral, he'd actually had the nerve—right in front of Cookie!—to brush his lips over her cheek and say, "Nice seeing you this morning."

Fortunately, Cookie had been so busy complaining about doctors and hospitals, he hadn't paid any attention to Jordan's nonsense—which was more than she could say for herself. It had taken a will of iron not to follow Jordan outside, but she'd managed to stop herself, refusing to give him the satisfaction.

And what would she have said, anyway? It wasn't as if she had any say in what the man did or didn't do with his life. If he wanted to move back to Five Corners and run a ranch, fine. When she got back to New York, she'd send him a plant, she decided. Something big and gawdy.

With thorns.

So she'd stayed in the kitchen, put Jordan out of her mind and visited with Cookie. Drank coffee and nibbled on pancakes and bacon, listened while the cook filled her in on the latest news. Doyle, one of the newest ranch hands, Cookie said, fancied himself a ladies' man and she should stay away from him. Elton, who'd been with Stone Ridge Stables for four years, was working on his third marriage and she should stay away from him, too. The town had hired a new sheriff after Neil Harbor, the old sheriff, got drunk on duty and shot his toe off, and talk was that Jody Sherman, who owned the hair salon, had offered the new sheriff free haircuts. Cookie had raised one thick, salt and pepper brow on the word "free," implying that the woman had been offering more than a haircut. He'd then told her to stay away from the sheriff, too.

And they said women were gossips.

But Alexis had only been half-listening to Cookie. As hard as she'd tried to stay focused, her mind had kept drifting to Jordan's comment, and her fingers had continually strayed to the spot where his mouth had touched her cheek.

For you.

When he turned and glanced up at her window, her pulse jumped and she ducked back. Dammit, the man had eyes in the back of his head! Frowning, she folded her arms and paced around the boxes she'd moved off her bed. Why was she hiding up here, anyway? She'd already brought her suitcase in and unpacked, she should be outside, enjoying the beautiful autumn weather instead of fussing over Jordan.

For you.

She moved back to the window, watched Trey and Jordan walk into the stables. He wasn't here for her, she told herself. He was simply messing with her mind. After eight years, surely he'd moved on. She certainly had. And if she thought about him on occasion, that was normal. After all, she'd had a crush on him most of her life, then a brief, though incredibly intense relationship. It stood to reason she'd think about him, have certain feelings for him, even if things hadn't worked out between them. Thankfully, she'd been smart enough to get out before she fell any harder for him. Before he consumed her.

She wouldn't give control like that to any man. She'd seen firsthand what that kind of love had done to her mother. It had obsessed her, and eventually driven her crazy. *I'm stronger than that,* Alexis thought. *I have to be.*

Eight years ago, she'd shed tears over Jordan, felt a pain like nothing she'd ever known. But she'd put those feelings, and Jordan, behind her, and she'd never cried over any man since.

"Allie!"

Alexis jumped at the sound of her sister's shout, then turned and rushed down the stairs. Kiera and Alaina were coming through the front door, their arms loaded with shopping bags.

Kiera dropped the packages on the hardwood floor and ran at Alexis, laughing as she threw her arms around her. Alaina joined them a moment later and they all hugged as one.

"You cut your hair!" Kiera pulled back. "I love it!"

"So do I." Alaina touched the ends brushing her twin's chin. "It's perfect for you."

"Trey didn't even notice," Alexis complained, dragging a hand over her scalp. She realized that Jordan hadn't commented on her new style, either. Not that it mattered, she thought quickly. Because it didn't. Not one little bit.

"And you." Alexis took Kiera's face in her hands. "My baby sister. Getting married."

"I can't believe it myself." Kiera blinked back her tears. "In five days I'll be Mrs. Sam Prescott."

"*Chef* Mrs. Sam Prescott," Alaina added proudly. "Our little sister is now officially executive chef at the famous Four Winds Hotel five star restaurant in Wolf River."

"Executive chef?" It was Alexis's turn to blink back tears. "When did this happen?"

"Three days ago," Kiera said, grinning. "And now that Alaina and D.J. have decided to have their wedding at the Four Winds, too, I'm going to design an entire menu just for them."

Alexis looked at her twin. "You didn't tell me you set a date."

"I'm sorry, we just decided on the second weekend in December." Alaina bit her lip. "But it's not set in stone, so if it's not good for you—"

"Don't be silly, of course it's good for me. Any time at all is wonderful." Shaking her head, she hugged both her sisters again. "Come on, the champagne's already on ice. And speaking of ice, let's have a look at your rings."

Two hands came up simultaneously and Alexis sucked in an admiring breath at the sparkling diamonds. Kiera's was an elegant emerald cut, Alaina's a more delicate oval. Both were at least a stunning two carats each. "Now that's what I'm talkin' about, girls. I haven't even met these men and I like them already."

Laughing, they all tumbled into the kitchen. Alexis popped open one of the two bottles of Cristal she'd brought from New York, filled three flutes she'd found in the back of a cupboard, and raised her glass. "To sisters."

They clinked glasses and sipped, then they were all talking at once.

"Please tell me my bridesmaid dress won't make me look like a poodle."

"It won't. Allie, I love your jeans."

"They haven't hit the stores yet. I'll get you both a pair."

"Get us that sweater while you're at it. It's gorgeous."

"A honeymoon in Paris. How romantic."

"Wait till you see the hotel chapel. It's beautiful."

When the conversation finally settled down and they all stopped trying to talk over each other, Alexis opened the second bottle of champagne and refilled their glasses.

"So what's it like, Allie?" Alaina brought her knees up and wrapped her arms around them. "Being an editor with a fancy New York magazine and having your own fashion column?"

"Such a bore." As if she were annoyed, Alexis tossed her head back. "Parties, fashion shows, endless shopping. Free clothes."

"So how much do you pay them to work there?" Kiera asked.

"Don't tell them, but I would," Alexis said. "Especially now that I can afford to."

"It's still surreal, isn't it?" Alaina shook her head solemnly. "Our whole lives, never having enough money, barely scraping by, then each of us suddenly inheriting all this money from a grandfather we never knew."

"Do we even know exactly how much it is?" Alexis asked. Last she'd heard, the accountant was still adding up the different accounts that had been earning interest for the past twenty-two years.

"Not yet," Alaina replied. "But it's probably enough to start your own magazine, if you wanted to."

A possibility to consider, Alexis thought, then

lifted her glass and looked at Kiera. "Or your own restaurant."

"Maybe one day," Kiera said, shaking her head. "But right now I've got everything I want. I'm just glad Trey will be able to expand the ranch the way he's always wanted to and we don't have to worry about Mom getting the best care."

A quiet settled over the room. They'd celebrated their good fortunes, avoided mentioning their mother, but they all knew it needed to be discussed. It was just so damn painful.

With a sigh, Alexis set her champagne glass down. "How is she?"

"Kiera and I went to the hospital yesterday to see her," Alaina said quietly. "She thought we were on our way to watch Trey play football and told us not to be out too late."

Helena Blackhawk had always lived in the past, Alexis thought sadly. One that she'd created in her mind. A fantasy world where the man she'd loved—the married man—hadn't abandoned her and her children. "I take it you haven't told her that you're both engaged and getting married?"

Kiera shook her head. "Her psychiatrist discouraged it. She has such a difficult time with any kind of change, and lately she'd been even worse. The doctor is experimenting with some new medications, though, so we're hoping they might help. I was even thinking I could postpone the wedding for a few weeks, wait and see if maybe she—"

"Don't even think about it." Alexis wagged at finger at Kiera, then Alaina, who had the same guilty look in her eyes. "Or you. You've both found wonderful men who obviously adore you and would do anything for you. If I'm half as lucky as you two, maybe we'll be celebrating for me in a few months."

Damn. Alexis quickly bit the inside of her lip and wished she could take that last part back. Obviously, the champagne had loosened her tongue, and she could only hope the comment would slip by unnoticed.

No such luck.

"You're dating someone?" Kiera asked.

"Alexis is always dating someone," Alaina said, but she'd leaned forward with interest.

"But she never mentions it." Kiera arched a brow. "Especially in the same sentence as the M word."

"I did not say the M word." Alexis did her best to casually backtrack. Lord, she wasn't ready for this conversation. "I simply said maybe, that's all. You two just have weddings on the brain."

"What's his name?" Alaina asked.

"Where did you meet him?" Kiera piped in.

Alexis sighed and shook her head. Her sisters would be like she-wolves circling in on prey. Women in love thought everyone else should be in love, too—or at least want to be in love. She wasn't, and didn't want to be.

When Trey and Jordan came stomping in from the mudroom off the kitchen, Alexis could have kissed them. Well, Trey, anyway, she amended silently.

Trey looked at the champagne bottles and glasses, then frowned at Jordan. "Looks like they're celebrating without us."

"Jordan!" Kiera jumped up and kissed him. "You made it! Please tell me this means you're coming to the wedding."

"Would I miss seeing my favorite girl get married?" Jordan pulled Kiera into a warm hug.

"Two-timer." Alaina kissed Jordan's cheek, then wrapped her arms around him, too. "I thought I was your favorite girl."

Jordan grinned at Alaina. "Your turn's in two months."

Alexis resisted rolling her eyes and downed the last of her champagne, though it seemed to have lost its bubble. She knew her sisters had always thought of Jordan as a second big brother and she knew that they assumed she'd felt the same way, though nothing could have been further from the truth.

If there was one thing she'd never had for Jordan, it was brotherly feelings.

"Sounds like it might be Alexis's turn coming up pretty soon, too." Kiera rooted in the cupboard for more glasses. "She was just starting to tell us about her new boyfriend."

When Jordan's glance swiveled toward her, Alexis gritted her teeth. Terrific. Just what she wanted. To discuss her new boyfriend with Jordan.

"Is that so?" Jordan lifted an interested brow. "She didn't mention him this morning."

Alexis tightened her fingers on the stem of her glass. She knew perfectly well his "this morning" comment was a reminder she'd been in bed with him earlier. "I don't believe the subject came up."

"Come on, sis, give." Kiera handed a glass

of champagne to Jordan and Trey. "At least tell us his name."

Dammit. With everyone looking at her, waiting for an answer, what choice did she have? "Matthew," she said evenly. "Matthew Langley."

"Matthew Langley?" Kiera's eyes narrowed in thought, then widened. "As in Matthew Langley, the entertainment reporter on channel ten?"

Unimpressed, Trey took a sip of his champagne and made a face. "Never heard of him."

"He's on channel six here." Alaina's voice was laced with awe. "Wasn't he voted one of the top ten best looking news men on television?"

Stunned, Alexis might have asked her sister how she knew that, but she didn't want to encourage the discussion. "We're here to talk about your weddings, not my love life."

"It must be serious," Kiera said, and looked at Alaina knowingly. "She's avoiding our questions."

Alaina nodded. "And she used the L word."

"It's an expression." Alexis pressed her lips tightly together and met Jordan's fixed gaze. "I'll let you know when it's serious."

"Do me a favor if you decide to get married, okay?" Trey set the champagne down and rooted inside the refrigerator for a beer. "Unlike your sisters here, spare me the torture of wearing a monkey suit. Just go to Vegas."

While Kiera and Alaina responded fervently to their brother's complaint, Alexis glanced at Jordan. His gaze met hers, and he lifted his champagne glass to her, then sipped.

With Trey under fire, Alexis saw her chance. She frowned at Jordan, then smoothly rose from her chair and escaped the kitchen without her sisters even noticing. With both Kiera and Alaina riled up, she figured she probably wouldn't even be missed for at least fifteen minutes, maybe longer. Plenty of time for her to put some distance between herself and Jordan and all that talk about boyfriends and weddings.

Quietly, she opened the front door, closed it behind her, then headed for her car. A drive would clear her head, she thought and slid behind the wheel, then remembered she'd had two glasses of champagne. She dropped her head back against the headrest, closed her eyes on a heavy sigh.

So much for her escape.

"Move over."

She jerked her head up as Jordan opened the driver's door, glared at him. "I will not."

"We need to talk, Alexis. Move over."

With him practically sitting on top of her, she hadn't much choice, and she scrambled over the center console with all the grace of a ballerina wearing flippers.

"Hey—" she complained when he started the engine, but he wasn't listening. He backed out smoothly, turned the car around and drove toward the highway. "Stop this car."

"No."

When the car tire hit a dip in the dirt road, Alexis fell against Jordan's shoulder, then quickly pushed herself away. "Jordan Grant, turn this car around right now."

"Not gonna happen. Whether you want to or not, we're going to talk." He spared her a sideways glance. "Put your seatbelt on."

She recognized that look in his eyes—the intense determination—and knew that outside of jumping from a moving car, she was trapped. She might be annoyed, but she wasn't stupid. Snapping her seatbelt on tight, she settled back in her seat and folded her arms, as if to dismiss him.

It didn't surprise her that he handled the sports car well. Jordan had always liked fast cars. In their senior year of high school, he and

Trey had spent most of their evenings tinkering on one engine or another. She'd never understood the fascination, but she'd hung around and watched anyway, and she'd learned the difference between a carburetor and a piston. When she'd turned fifteen, Jordan had taken her out driving once. All she could think about was how handsome he was, how close he was sitting to her. She'd been so nervous she'd ran his truck off the road into a ravine.

He hadn't let her drive again.

Now here they were, twelve years later, and dammit if she still wasn't thinking how handsome he was, how close he was sitting to her.

Dammit if he still wouldn't let her drive.

He turned east onto the highway, away from town. Other than woods and a neighboring ranch, there wasn't much in the direction he was heading. Except the lake, she thought and sat a little straighter. He wouldn't take her to the lake. The lake was their place. Where they'd gone to be alone. Where they'd talked and shared their dreams. Where they'd first made love.

"Do you have a destination in mind?" she asked with as much boredom as she could muster. "Or are you driving aimlessly?"

"I always know where I'm going, Allie," he said evenly. "You know that."

She did know. The problem had been she'd always known where she was going, too, and their paths had been in opposite directions.

Pretty much like now.

When he turned off the highway, there was no longer any doubt where he was driving to. Even for Jordan, this was callous. He knew perfectly well what the memories here were, knew that even eight years later, it would hurt her to come here.

"Why are you doing this?" she asked, angry with herself that he still had the ability to unearth emotions she'd buried long ago.

"I told you." He drove down the single lane dirt road lined with cypress. "We need to talk."

There was something in his tone, in the hard set of his jaw, that worried her. "About what?"

"This guy you're seeing—what's his name, Michael?"

"Matthew." She narrowed her eyes, knew that Jordan had intentionally gotten the name wrong. "Matthew Langley. Why do you want to know?"

"How serious are you?"

"None of your business," she said coolly. Still, in spite of her irritation that he'd abducted her and was now grilling her about Matthew, she had to admit she was curious. Curious why he would go to all this trouble, especially after all this time.

Not that Jordan needed a reason, she thought, other than he felt like it. That would be good enough reason for him. Or maybe in his caveman brain, after seeing her half-naked this morning, he thought he could bring her out here on the pretense of "talking," then conjure up a few old memories and see if he might get lucky.

Was he ever in for a surprise.

He pulled off the dirt road and the tires crunched over rock and leaves until he stopped in front of an outcropping of rocks where they used to climb. The lake was still today, and the warm, afternoon sun glistened off the calm surface. They'd skinny-dipped here under a full moon, made love on the shore, or sometimes they'd climb to the top of the rocks and lay out blankets, watch for shooting stars and make wishes.

When she was nineteen, for three months, she'd thought this place was heaven.

She looked at Jordan, and in spite of the warmth of the sun, a chill shivered over her skin and dread began to creep through her veins. "You have something to say, Jordan, just say it."

He stared at her for a moment, then nodded. "I never signed the annulment papers."

and stared at him from across her pillow. When
she could finally find her voice, her words
stilled his insides. For a moment, then softened
"I just met you. And so help me, nothing—"

Four

She went still. So still, Jordan doubted she was even breathing. He'd brought her out here because he'd been certain she would scream when he gave her the news. But then, when had Alexis ever done what he'd expected?

"What?" The single word was barely a whisper.

"I meant to sign them, of course." He was still waiting for her to take a breath. Or a swing. "I guess it just got away from me."

"It...got—" she did take a breath now, a deep, shuddering intake of air "—*away...from...you?*"

"I was in the middle of a merger and changing offices when the papers came and somehow they got lost in the shuffle."

Eyes wide, she swallowed. "You're telling me we're still married?"

"Technically?" He rubbed at the back of his neck. "Yes."

She stopped breathing again, kept her gaze on his as she fumbled for the door handle. He could have stopped her when she stepped out of the car, but he figured she needed a little space and a few minutes to absorb what he'd just told her. He watched her walk toward the lake, moving one foot woodenly in front of the other until she stood at the edge.

Overall, he thought that went rather well.

At the ranch, when Trey had teased her about getting married in Vegas, Jordan had seen her reaction. No one else but him would have noticed, or understood, the subtle stiffening of her shoulders, the slight tightening of her eyes. He knew exactly where her thoughts had flashed.

Vegas. Chapel of Cupid's Heart. Honeymoon suite.

Of course, the honeymoon hadn't lasted much longer than the ceremony, but that had been her decision, not his.

He looked at her now, standing on the shore of the lake, arms at her sides as she stared out over the glassy blue water. With a sigh, he stepped out of the car and approached cautiously.

If there was one thing he could predict about Alexis, it was that she was unpredictable.

He supposed her fiery temperament is what had caught his attention in the first place. If it had simply been those big blue eyes and dynamite figure, he could just as easily have fallen for Alaina. They were, after all, nearly identical in the looks department. When they were growing up, he'd always thought of them as the sisters he'd never had.

But that summer Alexis had come home from college, something happened. He suddenly couldn't look at her and think little sister anymore. All he could see was a woman. A grown, sensual female who'd made it clear she was just as interested in him as he was in her. He'd fought the feeling, made a point to stay away from the ranch, even skipped the Friday night poker game with Trey and some of the ranch hands.

But skipping that game had ended up being

his downfall. He'd gone into town that night instead, thinking he'd play some pool at the tavern, have a couple of beers, see if one of the waitresses there could take his mind off Alexis.

The tavern door hadn't even closed behind him when he saw Alexis leaning over a pool table, setting up her shot. He might have turned around and walked out if Jimmy Collins, Tyler Hicks and Bull Cooper hadn't all been staring so intently at her denim-clad backside. How the hell could he leave with those three idiots drooling over her?

He could still see her, her eyes flashing like blue fire when he'd told her he was taking her home. She'd argued that she'd come to town with Tammy and Jenny Campbell and she was leaving with them. Since neither Tammy or Jenny had been in sight, and Jordan had been in no mood to argue back, he'd simply picked Alexis up, tossed her over his shoulder, then tipped his hat to the other men and carried her out. No one had dared try and stop him.

No one but Alexis, of course.

She'd fought him, but it hadn't done her any good, of course. He didn't even bother to be gentle when he dumped her in the front seat of his truck, he just headed straight back toward her ranch.

She argued non-stop, and when he'd finally had enough of her mouth, he'd told her to shut up. She'd told him she'd shut up when she felt like shutting up and kept railing at him. Halfway home, he finally snapped. He'd pulled off the road, dragged her into his lap and kissed her.

That shut her up.

She'd tasted like honey and mint and though his mind told him to keep his hands off her, when she kissed him back, he stopped listening. From that moment on, there'd been no going back.

And the truth was, he hadn't wanted to go back.

"Allie."

She didn't turn when he moved beside her, just kept staring out across the lake. He frowned at her almost serene profile. He was used to her anger, knew how to handle her when she was in a snit. Quiet, calm Alexis, he didn't know what to do with.

Strangely, the longer she stayed silent, the more he felt his own anger build. "Dammit, Alexis. Say something."

"Say something?" She made a small sound of disbelief. "Eight years after the fact, you tell me that you never signed our annulment papers—"

"Your annulment papers." He moved in front of her, forced her to look at him. "Not mine."

"And that's why you never signed them?" Raising a brow, she met his gaze. "Because it was my idea, not yours?"

"I told you, they got lost in the chaos of the move."

"There is no chaos in your world, Jordan." She shook her head slowly. "Your world is orderly and neat and always in control. You don't lose anything."

I lost you, he nearly said, but stopped himself in time. He didn't want to tell her that anymore than she wanted to hear it. "I thought we should have at least given it a try."

"A try?" Her voice rose slightly. "Your idea of a try was me quitting school, moving to Dallas and setting up house, then popping out babies."

"That's not what happened." Rather than put his hands on her shoulders and shake her, he shoved them into his back pockets. "And you said you wanted children."

"After I finished school," she shot back. "After I'd worked for a couple of years."

"I suggested you didn't need to work." Lord, she was just as stubborn now as she'd been then.

"I was your husband. I had money, lots of it. I wanted to take care of you. What the hell was wrong with that?"

"You wanted to take care of me?" she asked quietly, furrowing her brow as if she'd never considered the possibility.

She closed her eyes on a long sigh, and when she opened them again, moved toward him, held his gaze with hers as she tentatively reached out to him. He stiffened when she placed her palms on his chest, felt his pulse quicken when her fingertips moved gently back and forth.

"If that's what you wanted," she murmured, "why didn't you just say so?"

"You never gave me a chance," he replied,

"So much time we wasted." She shook her head sadly, stared at him with those big blue eyes of hers. "If only I'd listened to you."

If he hadn't been so distracted by the soft tone of her voice, the heat of her fingertips and the closeness of her body, Jordan might have seen it coming. But because he hadn't, when she shoved him, he hadn't time to catch his balance or even better, take her with him. He stumbled, caught his boot on a rock and even as he fell back into the icy water, called himself an idiot.

"I don't need you to take care of me, Jordan Grant." Hands on her hips, she glared down at him. "I never did, and I never will."

With the grace of a queen, she turned and headed for the car. He'd barely picked himself up when she slid behind the wheel, started the engine, then spun the wheels and roared away.

Dripping wet from the waist down, he stared after her.

Son of a bitch.

He plucked his hat from the lake's edge, slapped it against his soaked jeans and jammed it on his head. It was a five mile walk back to the ranch. Not especially far, but distance wasn't the point here.

He'd tried to be nice. He'd even tried to be reasonable. He should have known neither would work. All's fair in love and war, he thought, and decided that when it came to Alexis Blackhawk, they were one and the same.

"You sure you don't want to come to town with us?" Alaina stuck her head in Trey's downstairs office that Alexis had temporarily—to Trey's annoyance—converted into a sewing room. "Cookie's grocery list isn't that long. We can have lunch in town, do the grocery shopping, and be back in a couple of hours."

"I'm fine." Alexis plucked a straight pin from the seam she'd stitched, then glanced up from the sewing machine. "Besides, with you both gone, I'll get our dresses finished sooner."

Kiera had argued that the Four Winds hotel tailor could have handled the last minute alterations for the bridesmaid dresses, but Alexis had insisted on doing them herself. She'd been sewing since she was twelve, had a degree in fashion, and from time to time, for fun, she'd even designed a few outfits herself. She could take in a seam blindfolded or fix a hem with one hand tied behind her back.

And besides, since shoving Jordan into the lake yesterday, she'd needed a project to keep her hands, and her mind, busy.

The image of him sitting waist deep in the water as she'd driven away had been the one bright spot of her day.

"Are you sure you'll be okay here by yourself, sis?" Alaina fidgeted at the door. "I can stay here with you, if you'd like. Kiera doesn't really need me at the store, and she's the only one who can decipher Cookie's shorthand, anyway. It's not like I'll be much help picking out the perfect roast or choosing the right wine."

"Neither one of us would be much help there." Alexis leaned back in Trey's leather desk chair and smiled at her sister. While Alaina's life had always been about horses and Alexis's had been about clothes, Kiera's passion had been food. "Kiera was the only person Cookie ever let in his kitchen."

"Only 'cause I wouldn't go away." Kiera came up beside Alaina and slipped an arm around her shoulders. "Come on, Allie. You've been holed up in here all morning. We're beginning to think you're intentionally avoiding us."

"Don't be ridiculous." Alexis felt the anxious tug in her gut, then rolled her eyes in exasperation. "Why in the world would I want to avoid you?"

When her sisters exchanged a brief look, the anxious tug in Alexis's gut turned to a pinch. If Jordan had said anything to them, so help her, she'd have to seriously hurt the man. She would make Jordan Grant's life so—

"We were talking so much about weddings yesterday and you went missing," Alaina admitted sheepishly. "Then last night at dinner you were so quiet, and we were worried that, well, maybe we were being…annoying."

Guilt sliced through Alexis. She'd been so wrapped up in her own emotions and Jordan, she hadn't even considered what her sisters were thinking. Ashamed of herself, Alexis stood and walked to her sisters, put one hand on Alaina's cheek, the other on Kiera's.

"Being here," she said quietly, "being with you both, talking about your weddings, sharing such a special time in your lives, would never, ever annoy me. I am so sorry if I made you think that."

"You've been acting a little strange." Kiera stuck her hands into the pockets of her slacks and shrugged one shoulder. "When you don't talk to us, we don't know what to think."

They were right, Alexis thought. How could they know what to think when she'd never told them anything about Jordan? She'd carefully hid that part of her life from them. From everyone. Maybe it was time to tell them. Not today, of course, but maybe after Kiera's wedding. Or better, when she and Sam got back from their honeymoon. But then Alaina's wedding was right behind, so maybe she should wait until after the first of the year, or—

"She's doing it again," Alaina said to Kiera, who cocked her head and nodded.

"I'm not doing anything," Alexis denied. "Now go already. I'll have these dresses done by the time you get back and you can both fuss over me and my strange behavior then."

With a gentle nudge, Alexis scooted her sisters from the doorway and went back to her sewing. When she heard the front door close a minute later, she stopped and listened to the sweet, blissful quiet. Jordan and Trey had left after breakfast to look at some yearlings in the south pasture and Cookie had begrudgingly limped off to the bunkhouse to rest his hip.

Satisfied that she was finally alone, if only for a little while, she sat back in the chair and dragged both hands through her hair.

She knew she had to tell her sisters the truth, knew it was the right thing to do, but she just didn't know how to actually do it. To look them in the eye and tell them she and Jordan had impulsively ran off to Vegas and gotten married eight years ago?

And were still married.

She was still trying to fully absorb the enormity of Jordan's announcement, had laid awake tossing and turning most of the night. How could he have done this to her? And why? They'd both made assumptions regarding married life before they'd gone to Vegas, and they'd both been terribly wrong. The only difference was she'd been able to admit it, and he hadn't.

As if Jordan Grant, Mr. I-Get-What-I-Want-When-I-Want-It, would ever sincerely admit he was wrong.

Still, even for Jordan, eight years was a long time.

Obviously, they were going to have to talk about their situation sometime between now and the wedding, but as far as she was concerned, the longer they waited, the better. After all this time, she reasoned, a few more days hardly mattered.

On a sigh, she laid her hands on the desk and stared at them. As clearly as if it were yesterday, she could see the gold wedding band Jordan had slipped on her finger. Their simple matching bands had been part of the "Double Deluxe" chapel service package. They'd laughed about it, and after he'd carried her over the threshold in their honeymoon suite, he'd kissed her and told her that he'd buy her a proper ring when they got to Dallas. She'd kissed him back and said, "You mean New York."

That had been the beginning of the end.

Closing her eyes, she dropped her hands into her lap. She hadn't looked back after she'd thrown the ring at him and walked out—hadn't dared look back. If she had, she knew she would have done anything he'd asked her to, given up everything for him. Every hope, every dream.

And yet, over the years, there'd been moments she'd wondered what if. What if she hadn't left? What if she'd gone to Dallas? If she'd had all those babies they'd talked about?

Would life have been so bad?

"Allie."

Her eyes popped open and she saw him standing in the doorway, arms folded over that broad chest of his, watching her. Damn him! Couldn't she have even a few minutes peace without the man showing up?

"I thought you were looking at yearlings."

"I'm back."

No kidding, was her first thought. That was one hell of an understatement. "I'm busy, Jordan."

Straightening her spine, she turned her attention to the dress in front of her and with a flick of her wrist, snapped the pressure foot onto the seam. She hated that he'd walked in on her at such a vulnerable moment. That she'd been thinking about him, about their elopement. About those damn rings.

Hoping he'd go away, she ignored him. Focused instead on the hum of the sewing machine and the seam she was stitching, determined not to let him rattle her. When he moved in front of her, she kept her eyes on her sewing.

"You're standing in my light," she complained without looking up.

He moved away, but the smug sense of victory she felt was cut short when her machine suddenly stopped. She glanced up, saw him holding the plug in his hand.

"We're going to talk, Alexis."

"This is hardly the time." She glanced nervously at the doorway. "Trey—"

"Is in the bunkhouse, having lunch with the hands. We're alone, Allie. Just you and me. We might not get another chance."

"You had eight years' worth of chance." She narrowed a look at him. "You show up here unexpected, spring this news on me, then expect me to sit here calmly and talk? Well, I'm not ready to talk."

He flicked the plug aside. "Get ready."

"You're still bossy, I see."

"And you're still stubborn."

"I'm stubborn?" She put a hand on her chest, then started to laugh. "That's a real hoot, Jordan. Maybe when you want to talk serious, you can come back and—"

"We're talking," he said firmly. "You want to keep wasting time arguing about it, fine."

"The only time I wasted was time spent married to you," she sniped.

If she'd hadn't looked away for a split second, she might have seen him move around the desk, might have even been able to avoid his hands before they'd closed around her arms. But she'd been too intent on being glib, had let her guard down for a split second, and she'd missed the warning signs.

"Take your hands off me." There wasn't much heat in her protest and she knew it. Worse, she knew that he knew it, too. The best she could manage was an indignant lift of her chin.

She could have fought him. Broken away, yelled at him, stormed off. Instinct told her to do just that. *Survival* told her do that. But here she stood, instead, her body pressed up against his, her breasts crushed against his chest, and every last bit of logic and reason dissipated like smoke in the wind.

And where there was smoke, so the saying went, there was fire.

She looked into his narrowed gaze and saw the flame there, felt it ignite her blood. No other man had ever sparked feelings in her like Jordan. Love, anger, frustration, joy. Passion. When she'd been with him, every emotion had intensified. Obviously, eight years hadn't changed that.

Excitement raced over her skin when his gaze dropped to her mouth. She couldn't breathe with him so close, couldn't think. "I thought you wanted to talk."

"We will."

"No," she managed to whisper when his mouth lowered to hers.

"Yes."

Despair washed over her when his lips touched hers. Despair and desperation and intense longing. She told herself to pull away from him, or at the very least, not to respond, not to feel. She might as well have told the sun not to rise.

So familiar, she thought. His touch, firm and solid, his taste, dark and heady. Her fingers curled tightly into the crisp cotton of his shirt. The heat of his skin radiated through her hands, up her arms, all the way down to her toes.

"Kiss me back," he murmured.

When she shook her head, he smiled against her mouth. "You know you want to."

When his lips brushed over her chin, she drew in a breath. "I do not."

"Fine. Don't kiss me back." He nipped at her jaw, trailed kisses down her neck. "I'll just enjoy this for both of us."

She was crumbling fast. Breaking down into tiny little pieces of need. When his mouth covered hers again and his tongue swept over her bottom lip, she shuddered. She hated that he had this power over her, that he could make her feel things she didn't want to feel.

The realization gripped hold of her and gave her the strength to resist him. Flattening her palms on his chest, she pushed. When he didn't budge, she pushed harder and turned her head away. "Stop."

For a long moment, he didn't move, then

slowly he dropped his hands from her arms and stepped back. "You're my wife, Alexis."

"Was your wife," she said, shaking her head. "I filed the annulment papers. Just because you didn't sign them doesn't change a thing."

"Like hell it doesn't." Irritation sharply edged his words and his voice rose. "Right or wrong, like it or not, you're still my wife."

She opened her mouth to argue, but something from the doorway—a slight movement, or maybe a sound—caught her attention. She froze, turned stiffly and felt her heart stop.

Damn.

Alaina and Kiera stood in the doorway, their eyes wide, jaws slack. All things considered, Alexis supposed she could have dealt with them finding out like this. They were her sisters, after all, and at some point she'd been going to tell them the truth, anyway.

What she couldn't deal with, and most certainly didn't want to face, was the man standing behind them.

Dear God, please tell me I'm hallucinating.

Matthew met her gaze, glanced at Jordan, then looked back to her again. "Hello, Alexis."

Five

Alexis felt the blood drain from her head, and when the room started to tilt, put a hand on the edge of the desk to steady herself. She wasn't hallucinating. She wasn't dreaming. The man she'd been dating for the past few weeks stood less than ten feet away, looking very polished in his tan slacks and white Ralph Lauren shirt.

The question was, how long had he been standing there?

Based on the hard set of his mouth and the burn of steel in his eyes, long enough.

"Matthew." She dragged a shaky hand through her hair. "How did you, where…"

"He was pulling off the highway, heading for the ranch." Kiera's voice was cheerful, though a bit strained. She glanced briefly at Jordan, swallowed, then turned her stunned gaze back to Alexis. "We practically ran into each other. Imagine that."

"You should have called and told me you were coming." Alexis made her best attempt at a smile, but since she wasn't certain her knees were strong enough yet, didn't dare move. "I would have picked you up from the airport."

"My meeting in Los Angeles was rescheduled, so I thought I'd surprise you. Seems that I succeeded." Matthew stepped into the room, moved toward Jordan and held out his hand. "Matthew Langley."

"Jordan Grant."

Alexis felt as if she were having an out of body experience as she watched the two men look each other in the eye and shake hands, wondered if this situation could possibly get any weirder.

Didn't want to know if it could.

"Must be awkward," Matthew said evenly. "Meeting your wife's boyfriend."

"No more awkward than meeting your girl-friend's husband," Jordan replied with a shrug.

"You are *not* my husband." When her voice cracked, Alexis cleared her throat and frantically searched for an explanation. Couldn't find one that made any sense. "Matthew, this isn't how it looks."

"So you're not married?" Matthew asked.

"Well, yes, sort of. Technically." Alexis dragged air into her lungs, felt the walls of Trey's suddenly crowded office closing in on her. "But it's really more of a misunderstanding."

"You mean you really are married?" Alaina asked incredulously. "You and Jordan? To each other?"

"*Were* married," Alexis quickly corrected, felt the beginning of a dull ache right behind her eyes. "Past tense. Briefly, a long time ago."

"This is a joke, right?" Kiera looked around the room. "There's a camera hidden here somewhere. We'll all watch it later and have a good laugh."

Alexis seriously doubted this would be a moment she would ever want to watch again or laugh at, let alone record. And why wasn't Jordan helping her out here? Why was he just standing there, looking so damn smug? If Matthew wasn't standing here, too, watching this little family drama-comedy unfold, Alexis swore she'd throw something at Jordan.

Better yet, Trey kept a gun in his safe, she remembered, and tried to recall the combination.

"So it's true?" Alaina glanced back and forth between Alexis and Jordan. "But how…when?"

"Eight years ago." Alexis wiped her damp palms on her jeans. "One of those crazy summer things. An impulsive trip to Las Vegas, an all-night chapel. We came to our senses a couple of hours later."

"You were only married a couple of hours?" Kiera asked.

"If that." Alexis shrugged one shoulder, gritted her teeth so she wouldn't scream. "We realized we'd made a mistake, I flew back to New York, Jordan went to Dallas, and we filed for an annulment. Until yesterday, we haven't even seen each other."

"He called you his wife." Though Matthew's comment was directed at Alexis, he was looking at Jordan, holding the other man's gaze. "Present tense."

"That's the funny part." Somehow, Alexis

managed a dry laugh, and it scraped like sand-paper on her throat. "There was a little glitch with the paperwork, and it seems that, officially, the annulment never actually went through."

"We're your sisters," Alaina said quietly, fur-rowing her brow. "How could you not tell us something like that?"

The hurt on Alaina's face and in her voice cut through Alexis like a dull knife. "I'm sorry. I should have told you—" she looked at Kiera "—both of you. But it just happened, and then it was over and it was easier to put behind me. Jordan and I agreed it was better not to tell anyone."

"Let's get one thing straight here." Jordan narrowed a dark look at Alexis. "For the record, I never agreed to anything. You asked me not to tell your family we eloped in Vegas, and reluc-tantly, I honored that request. Furthermore, *we* didn't make a mistake, or file for an annul-ment—you did."

"You wanted me to quit school and play housewife," Alexis snapped. "Cook your dinner and greet you at the door each night with a pink ribbon in my hair."

"I asked you to change schools, not quit,"

Jordan said. "And housewives don't play, they work damn hard, Alexis. I wanted you to build a home, a life with me, and I'll make no apologies for that."

She opened her mouth to respond, then closed it again. Damn him! Eight years was suddenly like yesterday and they were standing in the middle of a hotel suite, nose to nose, same old argument, same old opposing points of view.

The only difference, of course—a huge one—was that her sisters and her boyfriend were now standing here, too.

Shaking his head, Matthew looked at Jordan, then Alexis. "So you are still married, then."

"Matthew, I'm so sorry. This is just as big a shock to me," Alexis said, but when he lifted a brow, she sighed. "Okay, well maybe not quite as big a shock, but it's still a shock. After Kiera's wedding, as soon as I get back to New York, I'll make sure the paperwork is straightened out. *We'll* make sure." Alexis shot Jordan a heated glance. "Won't we?"

Jordan's mouth pressed into a hard line.

"Where is everybody?"

At the sound of Trey's voice from the other

room, Alexis froze, then exchanged nervous glances with her sisters.

"I take it Trey doesn't know about this, either?" Alaina whispered.

Alexis shook her head. "Of course not."

"Could we please not tell him until after my wedding?" Kiera worried her bottom lip. "He's already grumpy about having to wear a tux on Saturday, and as the bride, I'd really appreciate it if our brother isn't aggravated any further. Mr. Langley—" remembering her manners, Kiera smiled graciously at Matthew "—if you aren't busy, I'd love for you to come to the wedding. As my sister's guest, of course."

"I appreciate the offer." Matthew looked at Alexis. "How do you feel about that, hon?"

How did she feel? With every pair of eyes in the room turned on her, how could she feel?

Trapped.

The walls in the room just kept getting smaller and smaller, but somehow, Alexis managed to move beside Matthew, slip her arm into his and smile up at him. "I think it's wonderful."

"Maybe we should ask Jordan if it's okay with him." Matthew looked at Jordan. "Him being your husband—technically and all."

Alexis heard the challenge in Matthew's voice, could see it returned in Jordan's hard, steady gaze. Good grief, as if she hadn't had enough problems with one man, she thought miserably. Now she had to deal with two.

"Where the hell is everyone?" Trey yelled out again, louder this time.

Make that three men, Alexis decided, turned as her brother stuck his head in the doorway and frowned at everyone.

"Look who we found," Kiera exclaimed, her voice a little too bright, a little too high. "Alexis's boyfriend. Isn't this fun?"

Fun? Alexis could think of several words, not one of them even remotely resembling fun. The dull ache in her brain turned to a sharp pound, but somehow she managed to make it through the introductions and the strain of pretending she was thrilled Matthew had shown up.

If not for Jordan, she thought irritably, she would be thrilled. It was sweet of Matthew to come all this way and surprise her. Romantic, even. He was handsome, funny, understanding. Open-minded. Everything a woman could want. Everything she wanted.

It meant nothing that her lips were still

tingling from Jordan's kiss. That her skin was still humming.

Nothing.

She managed to keep the smile on her face when they all moved into the other room for something cold to drink. As soon as she could find a moment alone with Matthew, she'd be able to explain about her very brief marriage.

And once those annulment papers were finally signed, she thought, it would be as if her so-called marriage to Jordan Grant had never happened at all.

Cigar in one hand, glass of whisky in the other, Jordan leaned against the porch railing and watched the sun slowly drop behind the trees. He'd declined Trey's offer to join him and Matthew on a tour of the stables and paddocks, preferring instead the comfortable solitude of the early evening.

The deepening shadows brought an edge of autumn chill to the warm evening air, carried with it the scent of honeysuckle and late blooming roses from Alaina's garden. From the creek behind the house, bullfrogs croaked a throaty chorus, while inside the house, the sounds of female conversation and laughter mingled with the clack of plates and silverware being cleared from the table.

If he closed his eyes, he could almost be seventeen again, though he wouldn't be standing here on the porch. He'd be behind the barn, sneaking a beer and cigarette with Trey, hoping like hell that Helena Blackhawk didn't come flying around the corner, ranting about the sins of tobacco and alcohol leading to the more erotic depravity of the flesh.

As teenagers, he and Trey had prayed that was true. Women were wonderful, mysterious, sweet smelling creatures that occupied most of their thoughts and a great deal of their time. Opportunities to explore the female gender up close and personal were sought after with enthusiastic and competitive imagination.

Jordan smiled at the memory, remembered he'd once overheard Betty Rutfield tell Lucy Overton that between Trey Blackhawk and Jordan Grant, no man's daughter was safe in Stone Ridge.

Jordan had known that everyone in Stone Ridge had scratched their heads over Richard and Kitty Grant's son hanging around with that half-breed, wild Blackhawk boy. There'd also been talk that Trey's father hadn't really drowned saving a little boy's life, but was alive and well, living in Houston, working on a dude ranch.

There were other stories, too, Jordan remembered. That crazy Helena Blackhawk had killed her husband and buried him somewhere in the hills. Or that young Trey, abused by a drunken father, had murdered the man in his sleep one night and let the bears take care of the body.

Since William Blackhawk rarely came to town and wasn't friendly when he did, the locals didn't really care much one way or the other. Gossip and hearsay was usually much more interesting than reality, anyway, most folks figured.

Even Jordan hadn't known what the truth was until the day after he and Trey had graduated high school. Following the ceremony on the football field, Trey's mother had cried and kissed him, told him how proud his father would have been, how she wished her Willie could have seen his little boy all grown up.

The next morning, with all the parties and high school behind them, Jordan remembered sitting on the hood of Trey's old black truck, the last six pack of longnecks between them, watching the sun come up over the lake.

"My father isn't dead," Trey had said quietly, staring at the sunrise while he tipped a bottle to his mouth. "He lives in Wolf River with his wife and a son, owns one hundred thousand prime acres of ranchland and has more money than God."

Trey threw his bottle into the circle they'd drawn in the dirt several yards ago and it landed dead center. "My mother was William Blackhawk's dirty little secret. When he got tired of her and the half-breed brats he'd never wanted, he paid her off and never looked back. My mom's been telling that story so long about her poor Willie drowning trying to save a child, even she believes it."

Jordan stared at the bottle in his hand, then finished off the last of his beer and tossed it into the circle, as well. It landed beside Trey's, broke in two. "My mom's sleeping with my dad's lawyer and my dad is sleeping with his best friend's wife."

Trey said nothing for a long moment, but then he started to laugh. Quietly at first, then harder. Jordan joined him and before long they were both falling off the hood, rolling in the dirt.

They'd moved on with their lives. Jordan to

college, Trey running his family's ranch, but William Blackhawk was never mentioned again.

Not until a few weeks ago, when Trey called to tell him that he and his sisters had inherited a bucket load of money from a grandfather they'd never known, and a conservative figure for each of them, by the time they totaled all the accounts and interest, was somewhere in the twelve million dollar range.

That was one hell of a bucket.

Funny how life could change like that, Jordan thought. He blew a smoke ring, watched it dissipate. Blink of an eye. You're heading south, then wham!—you're headed north.

Just like his relationship with Alexis.

He heard the screen door close behind him and without turning, knew it was her. He'd been waiting for her, savored the knowledge that for once, she'd have to come to him.

Glass of red wine in her hand, she moved beside him, rested her arms on the railing while she stared out across the yard toward the paddocks where a hand worked with a roan mare.

"Nice evening," she said as nonchalantly as if she were plucking a piece of lint off that pretty blue sweater she had on.

"Uh, huh."

"Kiera's got apple cobbler cooling for dessert." Delicately, she sipped at her wine. "I swear I gained five pounds just smelling it."

He turned his head, studied her through the stream of smoke slowly drifting up from his cigar. "Looks good on you, Allie."

She slid a glance at him, let the silence between them linger while she watched a hawk soar overhead, then disappear into the distant treetops. "I thought dinner went well."

"Kiera's always been an impressive cook." He nodded in agreement. "And the fact that Cookie actually let her prepare the entire meal in his kitchen is even more impressive."

"Not without his supervision," Alexis said. "Or grumbling that all those fancy cooking schools had turned her into a snooty show-off. But I'm not talking about the meal, Jordan, and you know it."

"You mean because your boyfriend and your husband sat at the same dinner table without ripping each other's throats out?"

"You are not my husband." Her eyes flared, then she pressed her lips into a thin line. "But yes, I appreciate that you managed to be civil through the meal."

"Do I get a reward for good behavior?"

She tilted her head at him in that familiar stance of exasperation. "I'll see that you get an extra helping of cobbler."

"Next best thing to my first choice."

"Jordan—"

"Tell me about Wolf River," he said before she could scold him. "All those Blackhawk cousins you never knew about."

"Not much to say." She shrugged, took a sip of wine. "I haven't met any of them yet. Trey doesn't say much, but Kiera and Alaina think they're all wonderful. It's just hard to believe they've all been so welcoming, especially considering who our father was and all the people he hurt."

Jordan knew that William Blackhawk had been a first rate bastard, a man without a conscience or scruples. He'd cheated and lied, stolen money from his brothers, then sold out his own niece and nephews when their parents were killed. He'd lived a double life, one in Wolf River, one in Stone Ridge, and they'd both been equally vile. When the man died in a small plane crash three years ago, Jordan figured the world became a better place.

"Anyway—"Alexis drew in a deep breath

"—I'll meet them all soon enough. Even Dillon is coming to the wedding."

"Dillon?"

"Just when we thought it couldn't get any stranger or more complicated," she said, shaking her head, "and we find out William's son in Wolf River—Dillon—was fathered by William's brother. So he's not our half brother, like we thought, but a cousin."

Trey had already explained the confusing family tree, but Jordan was still trying to digest it all himself. He stared at the smoke circling up from his cigar. "You told Matthew all this?"

She stiffened, and her eyes snapped to his. "Why would I?"

"I got the feeling you were serious about him," he said casually.

"What if I am?" She tossed her head. "It's been eight years, Jordan. That's a long time."

"Maybe it's just exactly the right amount of time."

"We were kids," she said quietly. "Is it really so hard for you to admit we made a mistake?"

"I don't believe in mistakes, Allie." He wanted her to look at him, was certain he'd know the truth if he could just see her eyes.

"Every step we take, every stumble, every fall. Even when it's wrong, it's still right."

She did look at him now, and he saw the mixture of disbelief and mistrust on her face. "Since when did you become such a philosopher?"

"When did you become such a cynic?"

"I'm a realist," she argued. "A happy realist. For the first time in my life, I have everything I've ever wanted. An incredible home, a fantastic job, money. A relationship."

Jordan didn't miss the fact that Alexis hadn't mentioned Matthew until he'd walked out of the stables with Trey. Even then, her voice had lacked conviction. He wasn't sure if she was trying to convince him, or herself.

The sound of a cell phone interrupted the peaceful country setting, and Jordan watched Matthew answer his phone while Trey spoke to the hand working with the roan.

"Sign the papers, Jordan," Alexis said when Matthew slipped his phone back into his pocket and headed back to the house with Trey.

"What if I don't want to?"

Her breath seemed to catch, then her mouth flattened. "I have no idea what game it is you're playing with me, but I want you to stop."

He shook his head slowly. "No game."

"Game?" Trey's boot hit the bottom step of the porch stairs. "What game?"

"Alexis just asked me if the Rangers were playing tonight." Jordan blew out a stream of cigar smoke.

Matthew furrowed his brow. "I didn't know you liked baseball."

"She can't stand it." Trey stomped the dust off his boots. "Always said it was only one snore away from watching bass fishing."

"You don't know what I like, Trey Blackhawk," Alexis said indignantly. "It just so happens I watch a game now and then. Especially if the Mets are playing."

"That's great." Matthew moved beside her, slid a possessive arm around her shoulders. "I've got season box tickets I usually just give away. We'll go when we get home."

The smile on Alexis's face didn't reach her eyes. "I can't wait."

Jordan grinned at her, was certain the only thing she couldn't wait to do was box his ears for starting this.

"So—" she looked up at Matthew "—you ready for some dessert?"

"I'm afraid I'll have to take a raincheck," Matthew said with a sigh. "I just got a call from my producer. He's managed to finagle an interview for me with Phoebe Jansen."

Trey's head came up. "The movie star?"

Matthew nodded. "She's in New York for the next few days, promoting her new movie. Her manager called the station and set it up. I've got a two hour exclusive with her at 8:00 a.m. tomorrow."

"A two hour exclusive with Phoebe Jansen?" Alexis raised her brows. "Actors of that caliber rarely give more than a five minute cattle call interview."

"That's why as much as I'd like to stay—" he pulled her close and smiled down at her "—I've got a ten-thirty flight I just might make if I leave now. I'll fly back Saturday for the wedding. Miss me?"

When Matthew brushed Alexis's lips with his mouth, Jordan's hand tightened on his glass and he downed the contents, focused on the burn of the whisky in his throat rather than the heat of jealousy in his gut.

"Of course I'll miss you," Alexis pouted.

"It's the day after tomorrow," Trey said impatiently. "Can we go have dessert now?"

"How would you guys like an autographed photo of Phoebe?" Matthew offered. "Something to keep you company on a cold night?"

Jordan didn't miss Matthew's jab, but refused to rise to the bait. "Sure."

"Forget the picture." Trey opened the screen door and wiggled an eyebrow. "Ask her if she wants to be my date at the wedding."

"I'll see what I can do," Matthew said, then looked at Jordan. "How 'bout you? You want me to see if I can get you a date, too?"

"Not necessary." Jordan held Matthew's gaze, then he looked at Alexis. "I'm sure I can manage to find my own."

Matthew's lips hardened as he returned Jordan's stare, then he pulled Alexis closer. "I should go say my goodbyes."

Jordan lifted his glass. "See you Saturday."

Six

"I think I'm going to throw up."

"Don't you dare." Alexis closed the last tiny silk-covered white button at the neck of Kiera's wedding dress, tightened the inside clasp, then stepped beside her sister and slipped an arm around her corseted waist. "You don't have time. You have a hundred and fifty guests waiting for you to walk down the aisle in fifteen minutes."

Frowning, Kiera stared at their image in the dressing room mirror. "Not helping, sis."

"One hundred and fifty-five, to be exact,"

Alaina said, kneeling at Kiera's feet to straighten the hem of her dress. "At least, that's what the wedding planner told me a few minutes ago."

"Definitely not helping." Kiera put a shaky hand to her stomach and closed her eyes. "I can't do this."

"You can and you will." Alexis squeezed her sister's waist. "Now open your eyes, look at me and breathe. Alaina, you too, stand here with us."

Framing the bride in long gowns made of midnight blue silk, they all breathed together, slow and deep, until the color finally came back into Kiera's cheeks and her shoulders relaxed.

"Was it like this for you?" Kiera asked, holding her gaze steady with Alexis. "When you and Jordan got married, were your palms sweating and your heart racing and you thought you might jump out of your skin?"

Good Lord, of all the things she didn't want to talk about right now, Alexis thought, it was her own wedding. "Kiera, you can't compare what happened with Jordan and me, and besides, we really haven't got time for this right now."

"Please." Kiera reached out and grabbed Alexis's hand. "Please. It's not that I'm having any doubts about marrying Sam, I'm not. I just need to know if all these feelings are normal."

Alexis glanced from Kiera to Alaina, could see they were both waiting for an answer, both needed to know. Kiera, who was standing on the edge of the cliff, and Alaina, who was walking toward it, were, oddly enough, looking to her for some kind of reassurance.

"My heart was jumping around like a bouncy ball," Alexis said, squeezing Kiera's icy fingers. "My hands were shaking so bad I could hardly sign the marriage license."

It was all so vivid in her mind. The scent of red roses in the tiny chapel, the stained glass windows, the somber, soft-spoken minister. The memory stirred in her blood, tumbled in her stomach, and for a moment, she was back in that chapel, candles flickering all around them, the instrumental version of "I'll Always Love You" playing softly in the background.

"I thought I was going to faint," Alexis said quietly. "And then Jordan and I were looking into each other's eyes, saying our vows, and suddenly I felt a calm inside me, a certainty I'd never known before."

The words had come so easily, she remembered. Without hesitation, without doubt. At that moment, she never could have imagined she'd be alone three hours later, on a plane home.

She blinked, brought herself back to the present and saw both Alaina and Kiera staring at her. "What?"

"You're still in love with him," Kiera said, her eyes big and wide and full of amazement.

Cursing her loose tongue and wandering mind, Alexis plucked Kiera's bridal veil from the stand on the dressing table. "Don't be ridiculous."

"You are," Alaina agreed with Kiera. "Every time you say his name, you get that look in your eye, and when you two are in the same room, there's this feeling, you know, like a storm is coming."

"That's not love, sis." Shaking her head, Alexis fluffed the veil. "That's frustration. The man makes me crazy."

"Oh, I know *that* feeling." Kiera clasped her hands to her heart. "Sam makes me crazy, too. Especially when he pulls that, 'I'm the man and I know better than you routine.'"

"Oh, that's definitely D.J., too," Alaina said, smiling. "Sometimes I can't decide if I want to deck him or kiss him."

"Stop." Alexis took Kiera by the shoulders and made her stand still, then jabbed the comb of the veil into her sister's updo. "We're not talking about this anymore. Whatever happened between Jordan and me is ancient history. As soon as he signs the annulment papers, it will be as if we never even existed."

"You don't really mean—"

"Not one more word," Alexis cut Kiera off. "This is *your* wedding day. You look absolutely stunning and Sam is out there waiting for you right now."

"Alexis, I still don't think—"

They all turned at the quiet knock on the dressing room door. The wedding planner, a pretty blonde the Four Winds hotel had recently hired, opened the door and stuck her head in. "Five minutes," she announced, then disappeared again.

Kiera stilled. Wide-eyed, she stared at her reflection in the mirror while Alexis finished adjusting the veil and Alaina handed her a bouquet of white daylilies and pink roses.

"I'm getting married," Kiera whispered, then looked from Alaina to Alexis. Her eyes filled with tears. "I love him so much."

"No, no, no." Alexis blinked back the moisture in her own eyes. "Don't you dare cry now. If you start, we'll start, and we haven't got time to fix our makeup. Just tough it out at least until halfway through the ceremony, then you can let loose it you really have to."

Kiera swallowed hard, then drew in a deep breath and positioned her bouquet at her waist.

Handel's Water Music drifted in over the speakers, signaling the start of the ceremony. Smiling, the sisters all looked at each other.

"Ready?" Alexis asked.

A calm settled over Kiera's face. She lifted her chin and straightened. "Ready."

The Imperial Ballroom of the Four Winds Hotel in Wolf River shimmered. Votives flickered on burgundy satin tablecloths, white lights twinkled over the dance floor, champagne and chocolate flowed from bubbling fountains. Four-foot high pedestals of elegant white flowers graced every tabletop, and the sweet scent mixed with the aroma of Beef Wellington and chicken marsala while a ten piece band played a blend of soft blues and slow country western. A few guests made their way to the dance floor while others lingered over dinner, talking, laughing. Smiling.

Everyone except Jordan.

Nursing his second beer, he stood by the bar, watching Alexis. She sat beside Matthew at the bridal party table—the same table Jordan had been sitting at until ten minutes ago. Jordan had tolerated Matthew's presence throughout the meal, had even managed to endure the reporter's detailed recount of his interview with Phoebe Jansen, which had seemed to fascinate everyone at the table.

Everyone except him.

While Matthew had discussed a behind-the-scenes story about Phoebe's new film, Jordan had been mentally writing a script of his own, one in which an entertainment reporter from New York suddenly ends up missing in East Texas after taking a wrong turn off the highway. Alexis was the female lead in Jordan's movie—the runaway bride kidnapped by an escaped convict, ultimately rescued by a rogue FBI agent. Played by himself, of course. Jordan was still working out the details, but all in all, he was happy with the basic plot, especially the ending when the heroine shows her appreciation to the hero.

He'd spent a lot of time imagining that part.

Taking a long swallow of beer, he looked at Alexis, watched her unconsciously fingering the sapphire and diamond necklace at her throat while she sipped a glass of champagne. He thought about those soft fingers, what her hands felt like on his bare skin. Time hadn't diminished his memory. If anything, it seemed to accentuate it. It might as well have been yesterday they'd made love, he thought. He remembered every whispered plea, every moan, every touch. Like a rare, fine wine, he'd kept those sensations and the feelings associated with them bottled up.

He'd known that coming here, seeing her, would stir things up. In fact, he'd counted on it. But he hadn't realized to what degree—how strong and how sharp those feelings would be.

When he'd watched her walk down that aisle before Kiera, her blue gown shimmering like rain down her long, slender curves, his throat had closed up on him. He'd been robbed of oxygen, of coherent thought, and all he could think, all he could see, was Alexis.

Her face had been lit with joy; her eyes shimmered like her dress. She'd had that same look eight years ago, the day she'd stood before him and promised to love him, to be his wife. Forever. The thought was like a sucker punch to his gut.

And then the wedding march began and Jordan had forced his attention to Kiera. Like an angel, she'd floated into the chapel. He watched her take Trey's arm, who then presented her to Sam. There seemed to be a collective sigh from all the women in the chapel when the bride faced the groom, and when they exchanged their vows, the tissues came out and there wasn't a dry, female eye in the room.

When Sam slipped the ring on his bride's finger, Jordan's gaze turned to Alexis and their eyes met. She'd looked away, but not quickly enough. Not before he could see that she was remembering the ring he'd slipped on her finger, the vows they'd exchanged eight years ago. He also knew she'd never admit she was remembering.

Damn stubborn woman.

He watched Matthew touch Alexis's shoulder and lean in to whisper something in her ear. When she smiled and nodded, Jordan felt the growl roll deep in his throat.

"So what do you think of him?"

Eyes narrowed, Jordan turned sharply at the sound of Trey's voice. "What?"

"I like him, I guess." Trey signaled the bartender for a beer. "Which is good, since it looks like he's going to be around for a while."

"Says who?" Jordan snapped.

"That's what getting married is, Jordan." Trey furrowed his brow. "At least it's supposed to. Something you don't like about my sister's new husband I should know about?"

Damn. Trey had been talking about Sam, Jordan realized, cursing the fact he'd been caught off guard, and yet relieved at the same time because he'd nearly walked across the room and pummeled Alexis's *date*.

"I like Sam just fine." Jordan shrugged and glanced at the happy couple currently on the dance floor. "Why wouldn't I? Seems like a nice enough guy."

"Should have been there the first time we met." Trey tipped his beer to his lips. "I'll have to tell you about it some time. Now that you're moving back to Stone Ridge, I might actually see you more than once a year. Hell, I might even let you play poker with us on Fridays. Give me a few hands and I'll own your ranch."

"Or I'll own yours."

Trey rolled a shoulder and leaned back against the bar. "We could, you know."

"Could what?"

"A co-op," he said, leaning back against the bar. "Combine land and assets."

"Trey Blackhawk? Mr. Lone Wolf, combining land and assets? Wait—" Jordan tapped his ear "—I must have heard wrong."

Trey frowned, but took the ribbing in stride. "I've got the money to expand now, so why not? Our ranches touch on the east, I figure if we can get Ambrose Tucker's place on the south, we'd be a force to reckon with."

"Not a snowball's chance Ambrose will sell." Jordan shook his head. "And the old coot is too stubborn to ever die."

"Can't hurt to talk to him." Trey finished off his beer, sighed when he saw the wedding planner motion for him. "Think about it and get back to me."

When Trey walked off, Jordan did think about it, for all of three seconds, until he saw Alexis on the dance floor. At least she wasn't dancing with Matthew, he thought, but Alaina's fiancé, D.J.

Needing a distraction, Jordan glanced around

the dance floor, putting names to faces. The elegant redhead dressed in green silk was Grace, and her husband, Rand Blackhawk, was Trey's cousin, though the man looked more like a twin brother, Jordan thought. There were more Blackhawk cousins, Lucas, whose wife was a tall, stunning blonde named Julianna, and Clair, who was married to Jacob. Clair owned the Four Winds, and Jordan had heard that she'd been instrumental not only in bringing the estranged Blackhawk family together, but Sam and Kiera, as well. Clair was also pregnant, Jordan noted, watching her and Jacob dance alongside Alexis and D.J.

When Matthew suddenly reappeared and took Alexis in his arms and smiled at her, Jordan's hand tightened on his glass. Dammit, how much of this was he supposed to take?

But the real question was, how much *could* he take?

He lasted exactly fourteen minutes. Long enough for Trey to give a toast, long enough for cake to be served, long enough for the dance floor to fill up again. He polished off the rest of his beer, glanced around the room for Alexis. He'd kept his distance from her tonight, given her space, but now he wanted her in his arms, wanted to hold her close—Matthew be damned. If the dance floor was the only way, so be it. When he didn't see her, he frowned and looked for Matthew.

He didn't see him, either.

Jordan's frown darkened. They would have had to walk past him if they'd gone to the restrooms. They also would have had to walk past him if they'd gone out on the patio.

So where the hell were they?

He spotted them on the other side of the room, felt the cold knot in his gut tighten when he saw them walk out of the reception. Setting his teeth, he slapped his empty glass on the bar and started after them.

Seven

Alexis stood in front of the private elevator for the suite level of the hotel, impatiently pushed the already lit UP button. Regret flickered through her, but she'd made her decision, was certain it was the right one. And whether it was or wasn't, her motto had always been "Don't Look Back." It had gotten her through the difficult times, kept her spirit strong.

It would get her through tonight, too, she thought, drawing in a deep breath to reassure and calm herself. It had to.

"Alexis!"

She froze, didn't even turn at the sound of Jordan's angry voice from the other end of the marbled hallway. Dammit. She couldn't face him now, couldn't look at him, couldn't talk to him. As it was, she'd barely been able to take her eyes off him all night, couldn't stop thinking how handsome he looked in his black tuxedo, couldn't stop the unwanted rise of jealousy when she'd seen the single women staring at him, smiling at him.

She told herself it was just the stress of the past few days and watching her sister get married that had stirred up all these emotions inside her. Weddings did that to people. All that happily-ever-after business made a person's insides go soft and their brain turn to mush.

When Jordan called her name again, something close to panic gripped hold of her stomach, and she pushed the UP button again, cursed the slow elevator.

Relief poured through her when the doors slid blissfully open. She rushed inside and pressed the Close Door button, then turned and watched Jordan hurrying toward the elevator. His long legs quickly closed the distance between them, but when the doors began to close and she felt confident he wouldn't make it in time, she smiled at him and waggled her fingers.

Her smile disappeared when he managed to get a hand inside.

Jaw clenched, he stepped into the elevator car and pressed a button. The doors whisked smoothly shut and she felt the hum of the hydraulics ripple up through her toes, heard the sound of Carlos Santana's "Smooth" quietly filter through the overhead speakers.

When Jordan turned to face her, his eyes had the fierce look of a caged animal. She could barely breathe knowing she stood in that cage with him and there was no place to go, no place to run.

"Where do you think you're going?" he asked tightly.

His question caught her off guard, but she recovered quickly, determined to hold on at least until the elevator doors opened and she could escape. She summoned forth a bravado that her pounding heart belied and shot him an icy look. "Are you conducting a survey, or is it just idle curiosity?"

"Enough with the smart answers." He backed her into the corner. "Just answer the damn question."

"It's none of your business where I'm going. I do what I want, when I want, Jordan Grant, and I certainly don't need your permission."

"Good." He moved in closer, until his thighs touched hers. "Because you're not getting it."

Hold on, she told herself, though it felt like the longest elevator ride of her life. Chin up, she held his gaze, gave him a look that would have had any other man backing up. Any man but Jordan. Jaw set, eyes glinting, he stared right back.

The cold that had slithered through her a moment ago began to warm. He stood so close she could feel the heat of his body radiating through her dress, through her skin. Could smell the masculine scent of his aftershave, the scent of desire.

She wanted to push him away, but she couldn't bring herself to touch him, wasn't certain what she would do if she did. *Fine,* she thought, changing tactics. If she couldn't control the beast, she'd reason with him.

"This is ridiculous," she said with a heavy

sigh. "Jordan, please, it's been a long day. I'm tired. Whatever it is you have on your mind, can we just do this in the morning?"

"No."

She pressed her lips together, simply wasn't in the mood to argue. When the elevator finally stopped and the doors slid open, she said a silent prayer of relief—then gasped when he snatched her arm and pulled her down the hallway.

"Jordan!" She stumbled after him, struggling to stay on her feet and keep the strap of her purse on her shoulder. If she could have managed to snag one of her four-inch heels off, she would have beaned him with it.

When he stopped abruptly in front of one of the suites, she collided with him. "This isn't my room," she argued.

Ignoring her, he swiped his key card in the door and opened it, pulled her inside the room with him and shut the door. When he flipped the door latch, her heart slammed against her ribs.

Obviously, this was *his* room.

"What do you think you're doing, dragging me in here like some kind of Neanderthal?" She tried to pull her arm away, but he held on tight.

"If you think I'm going to stand by and do

nothing while you run off to meet your lover, then think again."

Her lover?

It took a moment for Jordan's words to sink in. Alexis might have laughed, but that would have diffused her anger, and she realized she needed the anger, needed something she could sink her teeth in and hold on to.

"What makes you think you can be out of my life for eight years, then just suddenly show up and boss me around?"

Why didn't it seem like eight years anymore? she wondered. Why did it feel as if it were yesterday? Same emotions, same heat, same argument?

"Because you're my wife," he shot back. "Eight minutes, eight hours, eight years, I don't give a damn. I *am* your husband."

"I signed the papers, Jordan." She lifted her chin, pointed it at him. "Just because you didn't, doesn't mean I'm bound to you."

"But you *are* bound to me." He dragged her roughly against him. "Marriage or no marriage. Papers or no papers. You always will be. That's what scares you so much, doesn't it, Allie?" he said tightly. "Because you know no matter how long you wait, or how long you fight it, you always will be."

"No." She didn't want to hear this. Wouldn't listen to him. "You can't keep me here. Someone will come looking for me. It's Kiera's wedding, for god sakes. You really want to make a scene?"

"The wedding is over, and by now, Kiera and Sam are in a limo on the way to the airport. But since you're so worried *someone* will come looking for you—" tightening his hold on her arm, he pulled her across the room "—let's just make a phone call and put someone's mind at rest, shall we?"

He picked up the receiver on the phone beside the living room sofa and punched the button for the front desk.

Alexis tried to grab the phone from him. "What are you—"

"Matthew Langley's room," Jordan said into the receiver.

"Jordan, stop it!" She managed to wrestle the phone from him and slam it back down. "Are you insane?"

"Obviously." His eyes narrowed to cold, black slits. "A sane man wouldn't be wasting his time standing here arguing with the most stubborn woman in the world. A sane man would have given up when that woman walked out on him. A sane man would have signed the damn papers and found another woman."

His words sucked the air from her lungs, and she stilled. Why did those words hurt? she wondered. How *could* they hurt after all this time?

"Why didn't you?" she asked, her voice strained and tight.

"If you have to ask why, it doesn't matter." He released her, and when she stumbled back, raked his hand through his thick hair and turned away, cursing. "Just go, Alexis. Get the hell out."

Run, her mind screamed.

Run fast and far.

But her heart whispered something entirely different, and she couldn't move. Could barely breathe.

If only those damn elevator doors had closed, she thought in despair.

"I wasn't going to Matthew's room." Her quiet admission hung in the silent air. "I was going to my room."

Jordan turned back, watched her with those dark, angry eyes, but said nothing.

"I broke it off with Matthew." She rubbed her arms, hoped she could hold herself together. "Yesterday."

"Yesterday?" Jordan's furrowed his brow. "But why would he—"

"Come to the wedding with me?" Embarrassed by her admission, she looked down at the plush beige carpet. "Because I asked him to."

He stepped toward her. "Why?"

"To keep you away." She closed her eyes, wasn't certain her knees would hold her much longer. "I figured if I could just make it through the wedding, then get through the night, I could go back to New York tomorrow, back to my life, without—"

When she stopped, he reached out, cupped her chin in his hand. "Without what?"

Opening her eyes, she lifted her gaze to his. Pride slipped away, leaving only raw, sheer need.

"Without doing this."

She closed that small space between them. That huge gap. Slid her hands up his broad chest, around his neck.

No more running.

Not tonight. Every last drop of denial, of resistance evaporated. *We're both insane,* she thought dimly. But there was only this moment, only Jordan. Insane or not, it simply didn't matter.

His arms circled her waist, pulled her fiercely against him. His mouth slammed down on hers. There was no need for seduction, no reason to coax. She wanted. He wanted. And they would both take.

His mouth stayed on hers when he scooped her up in his arms and carried her into the bedroom, kicking the door wide as they passed through. His taste, his scent, were all so wonderfully, erotically familiar to her. Fire raced back and forth over her skin, through her blood, and when his mouth dropped to her neck and nuzzled, she moaned.

The drapes were open, and moonlight filtered in through the soft white sheers covering the floor-to-ceiling windows, casting a silver glow across the room. Beside the bed, he lowered her slowly down the length of his hard, muscled body. Even as her feet touched the ground, she still felt as if she were floating on a cloud of intense pleasure. She slid her hands inside his tux jacket, slipped it off his broad shoulders, let it drop from her fingers, then lifted her gaze to meet his. Raw need glinted in his narrowed eyes, made her knees weak and her pulse jump.

Arms at her sides, she shivered, dropped her head back when he lowered his mouth and trailed kisses from one shoulder to the other. His hands slid around her waist, found the zipper of her dress and slowly tugged it down.

"I want you," he murmured, raising his head to gaze down at her.

"I want you, too." She drew in a breath when his fingers slipped the straps of her dress off her shoulders.

Blue silk shimmered to the floor, lay in a pool around her feet. What little she wore was black. Strapless bra, lacy thong, four-inch high heels. She stood before him, exhilarated, terrified, excited.

"You're even more beautiful than I remember." His throat was thick and rough, his eyes dark and narrowed. "And I have a fantastic memory."

His lips brushed her temple, her cheeks, then found her mouth again. His kiss was impatient, demanding, and she wrapped her arms around his neck, gasped when he dragged her down to the bed. Her hands moved over the rippling muscles of his shoulders, then slid down and searched for buttons, opened each one until her hands were inside his shirt on bare, hot skin.

He moved over her, pressed her deep into the soft mattress, caught her wrists in his hands and held them still while he tasted, moved down her neck to her breasts. It was almost too much. The heat of his breath on his skin, the feel of his mouth teasing, tempting, then nipping through silk, tugging on one beaded nipple, then the next, all of it made her crazy with desire. She moved under him, impatient, wanting to run her hands over him, touch him, but he held on to her wrists, arousing her all the more, frustrating her until she moaned in protest.

And still he held her prisoner, pinned her beneath him, holding her arms over her head while he explored her body with his mouth and tongue. She was gasping, squirming with need, and when he finally let loose of her wrists to cup her breasts, she moaned again, slid her hands over his shoulders and down his solid, wide chest.

She tugged at his shirt, wanting desperately to feel his skin against hers. Somehow, her bra had disappeared and his tongue stroked one hard nipple, then sucked. An arrow of intense heat shot between her legs and she moved against him, wanting him inside her, needing him inside her.

Pleading, moaning, she raked her fingernails over his scalp, then down his shoulders. His hands moved to her thighs, ripped the tiny strip of lace from her hips and tossed it aside, and his fingers trailed over her thighs, caressing the sensitive inside of her legs, then moving upward to the most sensitive spot of all.

Trembling, she arched upward when he touched her, felt the heat and cold collide. How had she lived without this? she wondered. Without him? When he stroked her, the question and every other thought flew from her mind. She could only feel. Pleasure coiled and tightened, and she thought she'd go mad wanting him inside her. When she could stand it no more, she pushed at him until they rolled and she was on top, grappling with his belt. They struggled together, until pants and shoes and clothing lay across the bed and floor and they were rolling again.

He rose over her, kneed her thighs apart and gripped her hips in his large hands. Breath held, heart hammering, she closed her eyes, thought she might die from the sheer need fisting her body.

"Look at me, Alexis," he said raggedly.

"Hurry—" struggling for every breath, she reached for him "—please hurry."

"Open your eyes and look at me," he demanded, catching her wrists and holding them at her sides. "Say my name."

She knew why he wanted her to do this, what his intention was, but it didn't matter. At this moment, she would have done anything he asked, she realized with dread. Anything. There was nothing she could refuse him.

Slowly, she opened her eyes, locked her gaze with his. "Jordan," she whispered, heard the desperate need in her own voice, and the frantic beat of her heart. "Make love to me, Jordan."

He moved his hands up her arms, held her tight and slid inside her.

Her world shifted; there was only this moment, only Jordan making love to her. She bowed her body upward, whispering his name again and again. Eight years of need and want slammed together and meshed tightly as one, then tighter still. Gasping, she wound her arms around his neck, needing him closer still, deeper.

They moved, wild and raw and crazy, matched each other stroke for stroke, both giving, both taking.

The combined force of the explosion was blinding, deafening. Pure white light blacking out everything but that one shattering moment of sheer ecstasy.

Aftershocks rippled between their bodies, left them both shuddering and gasping. Together, still holding tight to each other, they sank back into the bed.

When he could move again, Jordan rolled to his side, bringing Alexis with him. She lay beside him, limp as a rag doll, her body molding to him like soft clay. They were both still breathing hard, and the sound mixed with the heavy beating of their hearts.

He pulled her closer, pressed his lips to her damp shoulder and tasted the salt on her soft skin. When she shivered, he lifted his head. "Cold?"

Eyes still closed, she shook her head, but he pulled the sheet up over them, anyway. He figured she'd find an excuse to escape sooner or later, and he was determined it would be later.

Much later.

When her breath evened out and her heart slowed to a steady thud, he tucked a lock of tousled hair behind her ear, then ran his fingertips over her cheek. Her eyes, still glazed and heavy with desire, lifted to his.

"We always were pretty good at that," she murmured.

He kissed the tip of her nose. "We were good at other things, too."

"Yeah?" She pulled away from him, searched his face. "Like what?"

He'd never really thought about it. Never put their relationship under a microscope and analyzed it. "I don't know. Just being together."

"That's not an answer." She rose on an elbow, propped her head on hand and studied his face. "We fought too much."

"I loved fighting with you," he said. "Loved making up. Loved listening to you whisper on the phone in the middle of the night so no one would hear you. Those looks you'd sneak me when Trey and your sisters weren't watching. That sly smile that told me you'd be waiting for me at the lake."

There'd been times over the past eight years

when he'd wondered if that summer with Alexis had been a dream. It had all happened so fast, with such intensity, such need and passion, that it didn't seem possible. Love, marriage, annulment papers. How could all that be real? He'd told himself at least a hundred times it couldn't have been.

But looking at her now, laying here beside her, he knew it had been real. He knew that every moment with her had been more real, that he'd felt more alive, than the rest of his entire life.

"We were good together, Allie." Lightly, he ran a knuckle over her jaw. "Then and now."

She closed her eyes on a sigh and started to rise, but he held her down, kissed her until her resistance faded and she was once again pliant in his arms. He rolled to his side, bringing her with him, reached for the bedside lamp and turned it on.

"No light," she complained, shaking her head.

"I want to see you," he murmured, and slid a hand over her hip.

"Use your fantastic memory."

He snagged her hand when she tried to turn the light off, then circled the curve of her backside with his fingertips. "Tell me about this."

"It's a tattoo. Not much to tell."

"When did you get it?"

"Alaina and I—" She drew in a breath when he kissed her neck, moaned when he cupped her breast "—turned twenty-one. New Orleans."

He raised his head. "Alaina has a tattoo?"

"You tell another living soul and I'll kill you." She gasped when his mouth moved down her side. "We have a pact."

Her words didn't have a lot of heat, but her skin did and he tasted it, tasted the need. "A unicorn," he muttered, and nibbled. "A mythical flying creature definitely suits you."

She would have argued with him, but he moved over her, slid an arm around her waist and dragged her against him, kissed her hard and long and deep, until she finally gave up and kissed him back, her body quivering with need.

Abruptly he ended the kiss, rose over her, watched the rapid rise and fall of her chest, then the fluttering of her thick eyelashes as she opened her eyes and met his gaze.

"There's an elephant in here with us," he said raggedly. "Sooner or later, we are going to talk about it."

She stared at him for a long moment, nodded

slowly, then reached up and dragged his mouth back to hers. "I choose later."

It was a small victory, he thought, getting her to agree. But when they tumbled across the bed again, Jordan wasn't certain if it was his or hers.

Alexis woke to the glare of sun and the sound of water running in the bathroom. A bullet of panic shot through her and she bolted upright, looked at the bedside clock, then closed her eyes in relief. It was only eight thirty—not a lot of time, but just enough to get back to her room, shower, throw her clothes in her suitcase and get downstairs to meet the hotel car waiting to take her to the airport.

And with Jordan in the shower, she couldn't think of a better time to escape.

He'd be annoyed, she knew. But his time, she wasn't running. She'd promised him they'd talk about their "elephant" and she would. She just needed a little more time to think, to get used to the idea of him being back in her life. It wouldn't be easy, especially with him in Texas and her in New York. But she was willing to give it a try. Give them a try.

Dragging a hand through her hair, she sat,

winced at the pull of sore muscles. Lifting her arms, she stretched out the kinks and aches, then raised a brow when she noticed a bruise on her thigh.

Not that she was complaining. She figured she'd left a few bruises on Jordan herself.

Smiling, she glanced back at the bed, smoothed a hand over the disheveled sheets. Last night, she'd been so certain the morning would bring regrets. Certain she'd be calling herself ten shades of stupid, along with a flurry of other names that would best describe a complete absence of intelligence.

How strange it was—as hard as she tried—she couldn't muster up even a sliver of remorse, and the realization made her uneasy. She'd been so sure she'd made the right decision leaving Jordan. And now, here she sat, in his bed, her body still humming from making love with him, her mind still reeling, and she wasn't so sure anymore.

Spilled milk, she thought with a sigh and stared at the bathroom door. At the moment, the past wasn't her problem. The problem was now. Right now.

No matter what had happened before, no

matter how much time they'd spent apart, she knew she loved him. She'd tried to deny it, of course. To him, to herself. But it was the truth. More than life itself, she loved him. She always had. She always would.

But could she be married to him?

That was the real question.

When she heard the sound of Jordan's deep voice singing she snapped out of her musings and quickly glanced around the room for her clothes, frowned when she didn't see them.

She knew exactly where her dress had been last night—on the floor, next to the bed—where Jordan had taken it off of her. Her bra she wasn't so sure about, and her thong, well, that she was certain she wouldn't be wearing again. Even her shoes were gone, though she was pretty sure Jordan had tossed them on the floor at the foot of the bed, right next to his own shoes and socks.

Wrapping the sheet around her, she dropped on her hands and knees and looked under the bed. Nothing. Come to think of it—she glanced around the room again—she didn't see his clothes, either. She hurried to the closet and opened the doors.

Empty.

Eyes narrowed, she stared at the bathroom door. It didn't take a genius to realize he'd taken both his and her clothes in the bathroom with him. Carefully, slowly, she turned the doorknob.

Locked.

Damn you, Jordan Grant!

She took back every nice thought she'd had about him this morning. Now all she wanted to do was strangle him. He'd known she'd leave and this was his underhanded, double-dealing, black-hearted way of keeping her here while he took one of his twenty-minute showers.

She resisted the urge to kick at the door, ground her teeth together instead. Even with her sense of style and design, she couldn't do much with bed sheets, and the idea of strolling down the hallway wearing a white duvet cover or beige striped drapes was more than her pride would allow.

Cursing Jordan, she glanced around the room one more time, then tilted her head and smiled.

He wanted her clothes so bad, she thought and dropped the sheet on the floor. Fine.

He could keep them.

Eight

"Where shall I put these, Miss Blackhawk?"

Alexis glanced up from the column she'd been attempting to write for the January issue of *Impression,* sort of an out-with-the-old-in-with-the-new resolutions guide for cleaning out a closet. The writing hadn't been going so well. In fact—she swung around in her desk chair so she wouldn't have to look at her flashing curser on a blank screen—it hadn't been going at all.

Mary Margaret, Alexis's assistant, stood in the doorway, holding a tall vase of white roses and soft yellow Dendrobium orchids that blended in with Mary Margaret's pale blonde hair. When Mary Margaret moved into the room, Alexis allowed herself to lean forward and breathe in the sweet, delicate scent of the flowers, but because she knew they were from Jordan, she resisted touching them. She was still ticked off over his stunt at the hotel three days ago and she wasn't ready to accept anything from him just yet. Not a phone call, not flowers, not even the Belgium chocolates or basket of muffins he'd had delivered.

As if I could be worn down so easily with flowers and sweets, she thought firmly, though yesterday, she'd nearly buckled when a box of brownies from the Fudge Factor had arrived. The man was playing dirty, she thought, but he'd at least had the decency not to sign any of the cards. Her staff already had enough fuel for the firestorm of rumors sweeping the office.

She took another sniff of the roses, felt a chink in her armor, then shook it off. "You keep them," Alexis told her assistant.

"I'd love to." Behind her horn-rimmed glasses, Mary Margaret stared at the arrangement with big moon eyes. "But my desk is filled with the other flowers. So is Tiffany's, Scott's and Sandy's."

Alexis glanced through her window at the sea of floral arrangements in the outer office. They'd started coming Monday morning and hadn't stopped, and though there'd been quite a bit of drama and speculation over all the anonymous deliveries, Alexis hadn't said a word. Which only created more drama and speculation, of course. Most everyone thought she and Matthew had argued and broken up, or the opposite, they'd gotten engaged. But even those bold enough to ask her straight out had come away with nothing, and it was driving them crazy.

Which was where she'd been since Jordan had strolled back into her life, dammit.

"Throw them away, then," she said, but the look of horror on Mary Margaret's face had Alexis rolling her eyes. "All right, all right. Put them in the ladies' restroom."

Her assistant smiled at that idea and started to turn away, then quickly turned back, set the flowers on Alexis's desk and pulled a large, padded envelope out from under her arm. "Oh, I almost forgot. This just came for you, too."

Alexis saw the Texas postmark, then turned

back to her computer and squared her shoulders. "You can have it."

"But you don't even know what it is," Mary Margaret argued. "Aren't you curious?"

She glanced at the brown padded envelope. Okay, so maybe she was curious—just a little. With a sigh, she put her fingers to her keyboard and pretended the contents of the package didn't matter in the least. "You open it."

Mary Margaret's gray eyes lit. "You sure?"

Not really, but she shrugged anyway and started typing, though nothing that made any sense, watched from the corner of her eye when her assistant opened the envelope.

"It's a strapless bra." Brows raised, Mary Margaret held the strip of black lace up and stared at it. "Size—"

Alexis leaped from her chair and snagged the bra, then the envelope. *Damn you, Jordan.*

"Incoming," Tiffany yelled from the outer office, which had become the staff's announcement that another floral arrangement or package had arrived for Alexis.

Enough already! Alexis screamed mentally, stuffing the bra back into the envelope, terrified what might come next. She had half a mind to fly to Texas just so she could give the aggravating man a kick in the shins. She watched an oversized arrangement of pink roses moving toward her office and decided to stomp on every single long stemmed flower until—

She froze as the arrangement came closer, felt the blood drain from her face. Tall, muscular men in black Stetsons and Armani suits didn't deliver flowers.

Unless their name was Jordan Grant.

She watched him head directly toward her, saw everyone in the office staring at him, too, their jaws slack. If her knees hadn't frozen and her brain completely shut down, she would have slammed her office door and locked it.

Though a little voice in her head told her to pick up something—a stapler would do nicely— and throw it at him, she refused to give him the satisfaction and the staff a show. Instead, she drew in a calming breath and watched him step into her office.

"Mr. Grant," she purred, her voice the embodiment of complete composure. "What a surprise."

"I was in the neighborhood." He set the roses on top of a filing cabinet, then looked down at Mary Margaret and touched the tip of his Stetson.

Mary Margaret slowly tilted her head back and met Jordan's gaze. Her mouth dropped open.

Alexis resisted the temptation to roll her eyes—and to throw Jordan out. A route of indifference was the better path, she decided and kept her face and tone casual.

"Mary Margaret Muldoon—" Alexis glanced at her assistant "—Jordan Grant."

Jordan smiled and offered a hand. "A pleasure, Miss Muldoon."

Mary Margaret didn't move.

Alexis shook her head, almost felt sorry for her assistant. Jordan had always had that affect on women. Lord knew she hadn't been immune herself.

She still wasn't immune, she thought, looking at him now. In jeans and a T-shirt he could make a woman's heart stutter; wearing a suit and Stetson, he could make it stop.

Top it off with that damn smile of his, Alexis thought irritably, and there wasn't a female alive who stood a chance. Especially young, inexperienced secretaries from Katydid, Kansas.

"Mary Margaret," Alexis prompted.

The assistant looked at Alexis and blinked. "What?"

Alexis raised a brow.

"Oh. Oh!" Mary Margaret's cheeks turned as red as the blazer she wore and she looked back at Jordan, shoved her hand into his. "How do you do, Mr. Grant."

"Fine, thank you." Jordan's fingers closed over the assistant's small hand. "And please, just Jordan."

Mary Margaret's blush deepened and spread down her neck. "Can I get you, I mean, would you like someone, I mean something, or are you—"

"Mr. Grant is in a hurry," Alexis said through a forced smile.

"I've got a few minutes." Jordan let go of the assistant's hand. "Coffee, black, would be nice, if it's no trouble."

It *is* trouble, Alexis thought, and frowned at Jordan, but didn't dare make a scene.

"One cup of black coffee coming up." Efficient with a capital E, Mary Margaret sprang into action. "Decaf or regular? Croissant or muffin? We have blueberry, poppy seed, banana nut—"

"Just the coffee." Alexis moved to her office door, put her hand on the knob.

"Right." Mary Margaret glanced at Jordan again, who smiled even wider, and Alexis could all but hear the other woman's heart slam against her ribs. "Right away."

When her assistant hurried out of the office, Alexis calmly closed the door and faced Jordan. "What do you think you're doing?"

"If you're busy, don't mind me." He sat on the edge of her desk, glanced at the envelope she still held in her hand. "I see you got my package."

"I got it." She considered tossing it into the trash, just to make a statement, but it didn't matter how much money she had now—too many years of being broke had instilled a sense of financial prudence in her. "There are a couple of items missing."

"Not missing. I know exactly where they are. In fact—" he grinned "—I currently have my favorite close to my heart."

Alexis gasped when she realized there was only one article of clothing she'd left behind that was small enough to fit into his jacket pocket. "You didn't!"

He reached inside his suit lapel. "Would you like it back?"

"No!" She put out a hand, realized how loud she'd said the word, and how thin her office walls were. When she glanced over her shoulder, every head in the outer office quickly snapped back to their work. Eyes narrowed, she looked back at Jordan. "That's not funny."

"Sure it is." He slid his hand back out, empty, and folded his arms comfortably. "Just depends on where you're sitting."

"You're sitting on my desk." She tossed the envelope beside him. "What am I going to have to do to get you to leave?"

He raised a brow. "That's a loaded question."

"Jordan Grant—" Alexis sucked in a breath through her teeth "—so help me, I'm going to—"

"I'll leave if you do two things," he cut her off. "One, tell me how you got back to your room without your clothes."

He surprised her with such a simple request, one she was happy to oblige. "There were sheers behind the drapes. I made a sarong, then left a hefty tip for the maid to return them after you checked out. What's two?"

He chuckled. "You always were clever."

"What's two?" she persisted.

"Have dinner with me."

"Dinner?"

"Yeah, dinner. You and me." One corner of his mouth turned up. "I'm asking you out on a date, Allie. You know, like in a restaurant."

A date? Why should that make her pulse jump? she wondered. They'd slept together, even been married. Why did a date suddenly feel so intimate?

"I have a meeting."

"Cancel it."

"I can't."

"Then I'll wait."

She saw the determination in his eyes, the need, and her pulse wasn't just jumping now, it raced. She closed her eyes, drew in a deep, fortifying breath. "You can't just barge in here, Jordan, and expect me to drop everything."

"I don't expect you to drop anything, nor have I barged," he said quietly, his gaze somber now. "I've waited eight years, Allie. Eight long years."

She felt her resolve weakening. It *had* been eight long years, she thought, though she'd never even admitted that to herself. Self-preservation told her to stop this right now, to run, but she'd done that once and this was where it had brought her.

Right back to Jordan.

She couldn't think of a worse place to be having this conversation, or a worse time. Any second now Mary Margaret would be walking back in, not to mention the entire office was watching, holding their breath in anticipation.

But suddenly none of that mattered. She met Jordan's gaze and the rest of the world fell away. *Eight years.*

If there was any chance for them to have a future, any chance at all, she needed to know.

"Why?" she asked softly. "Why did you wait?"

"Pride at first," he admitted. "And anger. My idea of marriage was a wife at home, kids. I needed to know you would do that, for me, for our children."

She shook her head. "You demanded it."

He shrugged. "I suppose I did. I had to learn patience, Allie. Eight years without you taught me that."

"And the annulment papers?" Dammit, why were her hands shaking? "Why didn't you sign them?"

"I couldn't sign something that said we never existed, that you were never my wife." He rose, moved close to her. "You were and you are."

She backed up, couldn't think with him so close, saying these things. "What's changed?" she whispered. "We're still the same people. We want different things."

"I want you, Allie." He leaned down, brought his mouth close to her ear. "I want my wife."

"Here we are." Mary Margaret burst happily through the door, juggling a mug of black coffee and a basket of muffins. "I didn't know what to bring, so I—"

The assistant stopped, caught the look on Alexis's face, then glanced at Jordan and swallowed hard. "I'll, ah, just leave this on the desk."

When Mary Margaret hurried out and closed the door behind her, Alexis let out the breath she'd been holding, couldn't decide if she wanted to laugh or cry. Or both.

As if it might protect her heart, she folded her arms and glanced down at the floor, hating herself for being so weak. "I'll end my meeting early."

Jordan stood at the hotel penthouse window and stared down at the flashing lights of Times Square directly below him. Though he didn't mind doing business here, or even taking in the sights on occasion, he didn't understand this kind of life, this frenetic flow and non-stop crush of people and traffic. He was used to living in eight-thousand-square-foot houses, surrounded by twenty thousand acres.

A man needed space, he thought. Room to breathe.

He glanced at his watch, figured he had just enough time to make a quick phone call to his secretary before he left to meet Alexis at the restaurant. He'd made reservations at the exclusive Furbeir's, and sent a limo stocked with Dom Perignon and eight bouquets of long stemmed red roses to pick her up at her office. One bouquet for every year they'd been apart, he'd signed the card.

Remembering the look on her face when he'd walked into her office this afternoon made him smile. Underneath all her indignation and protests, he'd seen the pleasure in her eyes, had felt her soften when he'd told her he wanted her. She hadn't even argued with him when he'd told her she was his wife.

It was a start, he thought. A good one. Tonight, whatever it took, he'd hear her say it, too.

He turned at the knock on the door, knew it was

time for the evening housekeeping shift to come in and turn down the bed—a bed he intended to share with Alexis. If not tonight, then the next night, or the night after that. However long it took to get her to admit they belonged together.

At least this time if she ran away in the morning, he wouldn't have to get on a plane to chase after her.

He already had an image of her spread out on that big bed, her arms reaching for him, calling his name. Those fiery blue eyes glazed over with passion.

When he opened the door and those fiery blue eyes were staring into his, he felt the ground tilt under him. It took him a heartbeat to realize it actually *was* Alexis standing there.

She'd changed from the black business suit she'd worn earlier to a long sleeved burgundy sweater dress. The neckline plunged, the hem swirled around her knees. His throat turned to dust at the sight of her and when he took in the black stilettos and dainty silver ankle bracelet, his heart slammed against his ribcage.

She held an open bottle of champagne in one hand, two glasses in the other. Pink silk peeked out of an oversized black purse slung over her shoulder. Unless he missed his guess, it was lingerie, and he couldn't wait to see it on her almost as much as he couldn't wait to take it off.

"I felt like staying in," she breathed, her voice as smoky as her eyes. "I hope you don't mind."

She strolled past him, the scent of her reminding him of moonflowers and magic and everything that was Alexis. He watched her walk from the foyer to the bar, forgot to breathe when she sat on a barstool and crossed those long, killer legs of hers. When her dress slid several inches up her thighs, the blood in his upper body rushed south.

He closed the door.

Damn. He could never quite get his footing with this woman. Every time he thought he had the situation, and his emotions, under control, she'd throw him a curve ball. And the woman could throw one hell of a curve, he thought, sliding his gaze up her body.

She poured two glasses of champagne, held one out for him. He moved toward her, took the glass. "Are we celebrating?"

She narrowed her eyes in thought, then shook her head. "More like a suspension of hostility."

He clinked her glass with his, would take

whatever she would give him, even though he wanted more—so much more.

But he'd already waited eight years, he reasoned. He figured he could wait a few more days.

"I should be mad at you." Alexis sipped her champagne. "My office was in such a stir after you left, no one could concentrate. I had to reschedule our meeting."

"I'd say I was sorry—" He wanted to taste the bubbles that he knew would still be lingering in her mouth. "But it would be a lie."

"Honesty is good," she said with a nod. "A solid foundation for a relationship."

"Is that what we have?" He set his glass on the bar and moved closer. "A relationship?"

"I don't know what we have yet." She stared at her glass for a long moment. "Everything happens so fast with us, Jordan. Eight years ago. Now. I can't catch my breath when I'm with you. I can't think."

He took her glass from her hand, set it down, then lowered his head. "I don't want you to."

She laid her palm on his chest to stop him. "It frightens me, knowing you have that kind of power over me."

"Is that why you left me?" he asked quietly. "Because I frightened you?"

She nodded slowly. "You were older, experienced. Wealthy. You excited and terrified me all at the same time."

"Allie—"

"Honesty." She leveled her gaze with his. "Look me in the eye and tell me you didn't want everything your way. Tell me you didn't manipulate our marriage, then expect me to smile and nod like some kind of bobble-headed rich man's wife."

His first instinct was to deny it, but he knew that wasn't what she needed to hear. He laid his hand over hers, stroked her knuckles with his thumb.

"That was then," he said. "This is now. We're both older, both successful in business, and money certainly isn't an issue."

"No." She smiled. "That part is true."

"We're not the same people, Alexis." He cupped her chin in his hand, watched the blue of her eyes soften. "We can start over; just take it one day at a time. Figure out all the details as we go along."

"I want to believe that," she whispered. "I want to believe you."

"Believe this,"

He lowered his mouth to hers, kissed her gently, took his time tasting the champagne on her lips. He felt her resistance melt, knew that, at last, he'd broken through the wall she'd built to keep him out. It took every ounce of will-power he possessed not to rush her, not to make her agree right now that they belonged together. That she belonged to him.

He slid his hands down her shoulders, slanted his mouth over hers, deepening the kiss and ex-ploring the taste of her more deeply. With a soft moan, she opened to him, moved her hands inside his suit jacket, stirring the need and desire inside him.

"I like you in a tie." She reached out, took hold of the strip of red silk and pulled him close. "You know every woman in my office Googled you after you left this afternoon."

"Is that so?" He'd found a tasty little corner of her upturned mouth and nibbled there.

"I even caught Mary Margaret running a search on you," Alexis murmured, worked the knot on his tie loose. "I think she wants to have your babies."

He smiled at that, slid his hand down to cup

her breast, felt her tremble under his touch. "What about you, Allie? he asked. "Do you want to have my babies?"

Her fingers stilled, then she pulled the tie from his neck. "Maybe. Right now, I'm still deciding if I want you."

"You do." He trailed kisses over her jaw, nuzzled the spot under her ear that always made her moan. "Tell me you do."

"Yes." The tie slipped from her fingers. She drew in a breath and dropped her head back. "I do."

He slid his hands down to her knees, then up, under her dress, up her smooth, firm thighs. The image he'd had of her in his bed, naked, reaching for him, blew out of his mind. Now he wanted her here. Right here. On the barstool, on the floor. As long as it was now.

When she leaned back, draped her arms on the bar behind her, offering herself, he nearly lost it. Need pumped like wildfire through his veins, his heart pounded, in his chest, his throat, his head. He reached for his belt buckle, realized the pounding was also coming from the door.

He swore under his breath, furious at the interruption, but realizing that it was better now than five minutes from now.

"Housekeeping," he said raggedly. "Don't move."

He dragged a hand through his hair, moved toward the door and opened it. His heart screeched to a halt when he saw who was standing there.

Tall, blonde, face-on-every-magazine-cover, Phoebe Jansen.

Not now, he thought. Good God, not now.

"Hey, Jor." Dressed in a black Versace pantsuit, Phoebe breezed past him. "Sorry I didn't call. I just got in from drinks with Eve. She's hounding me to take that part I told you about."

"Phoebe—" Jordan avoided looking at Alexis "—this really isn't a good time."

"Don't worry, hon. I'm not staying." Smiling, Phoebe leaned in and kissed his cheek. "This is just the first time I've had to thank you for setting up the interview with Matthew. If I'd have known how hot the guy is, I would have done it without you asking me."

Just put a fork in me, Jordan thought. He knew he was cooked and about to be eaten, could feel the heat radiating from the direction of the bar. He put a hand on Phoebe's shoulder and herded her back toward the door. "Let's talk later, Pheeb."

"I'm serious, Jordan." Phoebe pulled away. "I really like this guy. I think I may have an affair with him."

Jordan wasn't certain if this could get any worse, but when Alexis stepped into the foyer, he suspected it not only could, it would.

Phoebe's brow lifted when she spotted the other woman, and she glanced back at Jordan, her face apologetic. "Sorry. I didn't realize you had company. I'll just be on my—"

"Were you talking about Matthew Langley?" Alexis asked, her voice cool and even.

"Do you know him?" Worried now, Phoebe stared at Alexis. "'Cause I was kidding about the affair. I mean, I just met him. Jordan asked me to do the interview, so I did, as a favor. For a friend."

"You and Jordan are friends." Alexis slid a frosty gaze at Jordan. "He never mentioned that."

"That's all we are." Misreading Alexis's icy tone for jealousy, Phoebe did her best to reassure the other woman. "Really. Just friends."

"And it was Jordan who arranged the interview with Matthew?" Icecaps were forming on

Alexis's words. "The interview that had to happen last Thursday, the exclusive, two-hour, last-minute interview."

Phoebe glanced nervously between Alexis and Jordan, not sure what to say. "I better go."

"No." Alexis slipped the strap of her purse onto her shoulder. "I'm the one who's leaving."

Jordan recognized the look in Alexis's eyes, the hard set of her jaw. He knew there was absolutely nothing he could say to her right now, nothing she would listen to or hear. Short of tying the woman up—and for a long second he seriously considered the possibility—there was no way in hell he could make her stay.

She paused in front of him, narrowed her eyes as she met his gaze. "Sign the papers, Jordan."

She turned then, and white-knuckled, his gut twisting with frustration, he watched her walk through the door and out of his life.

Nine

Muscles straining, arms shaking, Jordan lay on his back and forced the bar into one more set. The extra twenty pound weights he'd added this past week had honed and strengthened his body, but had done little to help his mind. The fierce urge to spill blood gripped him like a fist.

When he lost count, he swore and started over.

New York had been a fiasco.

Seven days ago, he'd nearly convinced Alexis that they belonged together. Had come so damn close. He'd even gotten her to think about babies, for god sakes. In the blink of an eye, it all vanished like smoke in the wind. Alexis, marriage, children. Everything he wanted.

Just thinking about it had him forcing one more set with the weights, determined to sweat out the image of her walking away.

Phoebe had felt awful that her timing had been so incredibly bad; she'd also been mortified that she'd teased about having an affair with the man. She'd offered to talk to Alexis, but Jordan had nixed that idea. He saw nothing positive coming out of the two women sitting down to "chat." As it was, Alexis would probably never speak to him again, anyway. Especially after all that talk about "honesty."

He would have told her about the thing with Matthew, dammit. Eventually. It wasn't really dishonest. It wasn't like she really needed to know he'd arranged for Matthew to get the interview the Phoebe. Phoebe hadn't minded doing a favor for an old friend.

And what was so bad about it, anyway? Grunting, he heaved the weight up again. Matthew got a great interview with Hollywood's hottest female film star. Hell, he'd done the guy a favor.

Breathing hard, Jordan dropped the weight into its holder, sat on the bench and stared at his reflection in the surrounding mirrors. Sweat ran down his face and back, soaked his T-shirt. He hadn't shaved in four days or used a comb in two.

He frowned darkly at himself. What the hell did it matter?

"You look like hell."

Scowling, Jordan looked up, caught the towel that Trey threw at him. "I'm busy."

"This how you city boys keep from going soft?" Tipping his black Stetson back, Trey glanced around the fully equipped gym.

"You wanna pump something other than your jaw, Blackhawk?" Jordan dragged the towel over his neck. "I'll spot you at two-twenty."

"Shoot, I pick up calves weigh more'n that." Trey lifted a seventy-five pound free weight and curled it as easy as a piece of foam. "Speaking of, I've got fifty head you can take off my hands, dirt cheap, if you want. That is, if you ever plan on owning a real ranch."

Jordan's hand tightened on the towel. "What the hell is that supposed to mean?"

"Most ranchers with land like this have some

kind of livestock. You know, horses, cows." Trey curled the weight again in one smooth motion. "Unless you're planning on raising hay."

"You got a better reason to come all the way over here other than annoy me?" Jordan asked irritably.

"Yep." Trey set the weight down and moved to the punching bag, gave it a couple of jabs. "The annoying part is just a bonus."

"Dammit, Trey, I'm not in the mood."

"I suggest you get in the mood." Trey threw a solid right punch into the bag. "Lisa Jefferies and Sue Ann Potter are on their way here, bringing us dinner."

Jordan's head came up. "What?"

"Lisa called and invited me to a housewarming meal to welcome you back to Stone Ridge. They'll be here at seven."

Cursing, Jordan snatched his watch from the hook he'd draped it on. It was six-thirty. "Why the hell didn't you call me?"

"I did." Trey danced on his toes, feigned a left and cut with his right. "You should answer your phone."

After six calls from his office in Dallas, four from his refinery in Midland, then two from his accountant, Jordan had unplugged his landline and turned off his cell.

"You entertain them," he said, shaking his head. "I'm busy."

"Doing what?" Trey slammed a fist into the bag. "Signing my sister's annulment papers?"

Jordan stilled, then slowly narrowed a gaze at Trey. "What did you say?"

"You heard me."

"She told you?"

"Alexis tell me anything?" Trey gave the bag a hard right. "Hell, no."

Jordan felt as if he'd taken Trey's punch directly to his gut "Then how—when did you—"

"I've always known." Trey straightened and loosened his fists, shook out his shoulders. "I knew the summer it started, the Vegas wedding, even the annulment. Only reason I let it go on without saying anything was 'cause it was you. Anyone else would be picking their teeth out of their tonsils."

"Why didn't you say anything?" Jordan stared at Trey. "All these years, and not one word?"

"I could say the same about you." Trey stared at Jordan, his gaze dark and serious. "And if I'd ever thought for one second you intended to hurt her, friend or not, I'd have to lay you out."

"You could try, I guess." Jordan nodded, and though he didn't like it, understood where Trey was coming from. "It doesn't matter now, anyway. She won't even talk to me."

"Because of the Phoebe Jansen interview?"

Dumbfounded, Jordan stared at Trey. "How the hell do you know all this?"

"I figured that one out myself." Trey folded his arms and leaned back against a treadmill. "I knew you'd dated Phoebe a few years back, right before she went big. I seriously doubted it was a coincidence when Matthew suddenly had to leave for an interview with her right before the wedding. I'm guessing Alexis found out when you were in New York."

"She's my wife, dammit." Jordan dragged his hands through his damp hair. "I'll be damned if I'll look the other way while she plays footsies with some other guy."

"You looked the other way for eight years," Trey pointed out.

"No." Jordan shook his head and let out a breath. "God, she'll kill me for sure if she finds out, but I've always known what she was doing, kept an eye on who she was with. Matthew's the first guy that I thought might be serious."

"So you decided it was time to convince Alexis she needed to come to her senses and settle down with you?" Trey lifted a brow. "Man, I would have loved to see the look on her face when you told her you were still married. Did she hit you?"

"She pushed me in the lake," Jordan admitted reluctantly.

"That's Alexis," Trey said, nodding. "Never could rein her in. She always did the opposite of what I wanted, just to prove she could. The night William Blackhawk packed up his things and walked out on us, I told her to stay upstairs. She was only eight, but would she listen to me? Hell, no."

No one in the Blackhawk house had ever discussed what happened—what really happened—the night William Blackhawk left. A muscle jumped in Trey's jaw, and his dark eyes narrowed, staring blindly at his reflection in the mirror.

"My mom was hysterical," Trey said. "Begging my father not to go. I didn't give a damn, I hated him. Kiera was too little to understand or even remember, but she was crying anyway, so Alaina held her, comforted her. Alexis just paced, kept saying that our daddy wasn't really leaving and never coming back. She said that daddies didn't do that."

It wasn't difficult for Jordan to imagine Alexis at eight years old, her chin lifted, her little back held straight, determined that her will alone would make her world be exactly as she willed it to be. It was that fierce resolve and unwavering belief in herself that had drawn him to her in the first place.

"I should have known she wouldn't stay put. Alexis never listened to anyone." Trey's eyes turned to black stone. "It was my fault, what happened to her."

Jordan's hands tightened on the towel. "What happened?"

"When the yelling got louder, I went downstairs," Trey continued. "Found my mother huddled in the corner of William's office while he finished clearing out his desk. He told me to get out, I refused. It would have come to blows right there except Alexis came flying in the room. Before I could stop her, she'd flung herself at William, grabbed on to his leg, pleading with him not to go, that she'd be good if he stayed, she'd mind him and do all her chores. He shook her off like a piece of dirt."

It was like a fist around his gut, around his heart, and Jordan couldn't stop the thought that if William Blackhawk were still alive, he'd want to kill him himself.

"I managed to get one swing at him," Trey said, satisfaction and hatred glinting in his eyes. "But I was only fourteen and he was a big man. He laid me flat and walked out."

The curse, raw and gritty, shuddered out with Jordan's breath. "She never said anything to me. Not a word."

"My mother isn't the only one who lives in denial." Trey rolled a shoulder, then sighed as he straightened. "Might as well sign those papers and be done with it, Jordan. That's what Alexis wants, you might as well give it to her."

"What the hell kind of thing is that to say?" Anger narrowed Jordan's eyes. "She's my wife."

"She doesn't seem to think so." Trey shrugged. "Once that girl makes a decision, there's just no changing her mind. Why don't you just go shower and we'll have us a nice evening with Lisa and Sue Ann?"

"Why don't you shut up." Jordan threw the towel at Trey and turned. "Damn you, Trey, just shut the hell up and get out of my house."

"Hey," Trey yelled after Jordan when he stomped out of the gym. "What about Lisa and Sue Ann?"

"Not my problem," Jordan shot back over his shoulder and headed for the shower.

At the moment, he had a much bigger, much more important problem to deal with.

Halfway home, the rain started to fall.

It didn't matter to Alexis. The walk from her office to her new apartment was only seven blocks, and after twelve hours sitting at her computer, it felt good to stretch her legs and clear her mind. It was more of a mist than a real rain, anyway, she thought, just enough to dampen the streets and freshen the air. Fall had moved into New York City these past few days, but no one seemed to mind the chill in the air. Joggers still ran in the park wearing T-shirts, nannies pushed strollers, vendors hawked their wares.

The world didn't stop because of one broken heart.

On the outside, Alexis thought she probably

looked like any other New Yorker coming home from work. She moved with the flow of the people on the sidewalks, kept her gaze straight ahead, her face impassionate. On the outside, she looked like she knew exactly where she was going, exactly what she'd do when she got there.

On the inside, she felt like shattered glass. Every breath, every beat of her heart, cut a little sharper, a little deeper.

It hadn't been easy, keeping up this front for the past week. She'd seen the curious glances, heard the whispers. There were hounds in the office, and they could smell weakness, would pounce at the first scent. She'd busted her butt to get where she was, to earn the respect of her peers. Sniveling around the office, all weepy and despondent over a man, was more than weak, she thought. It was pathetic.

She preferred the privacy of her own home, lights out, under the covers, to cry her eyes out.

All these years she'd convinced herself they didn't belong together, that they were completely wrong for each other, the chasm separating them too deep and too wide. She'd been angry enough at first, self-righteous, and those feelings had kept her sane. Kept her from running back into his arms and giving up everything she'd ever dreamed.

Across the street from her apartment house, she stopped, looked at the fancy, forest-green awning, the uniformed doorman, the elegant glass doors. She'd closed escrow and moved in four days ago. Sixteen hundred square feet overlooking Central Park. Marble bathrooms, sleek granite kitchen counters, twelve-foot ceilings and two fireplaces. She hadn't opened one box yet, hadn't hung up her clothes or even put sheets on the bed.

Her big, empty bed.

People would kill for everything she had. The job, the house, the money. She should be dancing with joy, running through the park, skipping in the fountains. Why the hell was she standing out here, in the middle of the sidewalk, in the rain, feeling so completely and utterly alone?

So completely and utterly miserable.

Because she loved him. She *loved* him, dammit. Beyond life itself. Beyond every painful breath and beat of her heart, she loved him.

She watched the rain drops slide down her

black cashmere coat, heard the cars passing, the bump of music from an unseen radio. All she needed to do was cross the street. Pick one foot up and put it in front of the other. Just keep moving. Why was that suddenly so difficult?

People walked around her. A man dragging three Pomeranians on leashes. Two teenagers talking, not to each other, but on their cell phones. A businessman flagging down a taxi. Daily routines, she thought. Everyone going about their mundane, ordinary, run-of-the-mill activities.

And she couldn't even make herself walk thirty feet to her apartment entrance.

The rain increased, but she didn't care. Closing her eyes, she sat on a park bench. Go inside, a voice of reason chastised her. Shut up, she replied.

She didn't want reason anymore. Didn't want logic.

She wanted Jordan.

She didn't want to want him. But she did.

He'd refused to sign the annulment papers, created turmoil at her office, used Phoebe to get Matthew out of the way. And still, she loved him.

Honesty, she thought with a sigh. There was hers.

From the park, she heard children laughing, a mother's warning not to step in the puddles, then the distinct plop of small feet splashing. She turned toward the sound and opened her eyes, almost smiled at the four little boys jumping in the pooling water.

"Mind if I share your bench?"

When she turned, it was her heart jumping.

Jordan.

She blinked, afraid that she really had gone crazy, and this was her imagination messing with him mind. She almost reached out to touch him, just to be certain.

When he sat down beside her and leveled his gaze with hers, she didn't need to touch him to know he was real. It was Jordan, no question about it. He looked a little tired, she thought, noting the tension crinkling the corners of his deep green eyes.

He looked wonderful.

She was still trying to find her voice when he spoke.

"I signed the papers today and filed them, Allie," he said quietly. "Tomorrow morning you'll no longer be a married woman."

Her heart, the little pieces that were left of it,

dropped. She stared at him. He'd done it. He'd really done it. Wasn't this what she wanted? What she'd asked him for? What she'd insisted on? Be careful what you wish for... The words flashed into her brain, bounced around like pinballs. She now had everything she'd ever wanted and realized it wasn't what she wanted at all.

For the first time in her life, she understood what her mother had felt. Why she'd gone crazy. Love could do that to a person, Alexis thought. Was doing it to her right now.

But she wouldn't fall apart here. Not in front of Jordan, in front of the world. She still had her pride—a thread, and she was hanging on to it for dear life. All she had to do was stand, say goodbye, and walk those thirty feet across the street to her big, beautiful apartment.

And she would. In just another minute, as soon as she was certain her knees would hold her.

She swallowed hard, held her chin up. "It was hardly necessary for you to come all the way to New York to tell me that."

He shrugged. "Some things need to be said in person."

"How civil of you." She managed to stand, forced the corners of her mouth upward and tried her hand at being cheeky. "Maybe we can be friends, Jordan, now that we're not married."

He kept his gaze on hers, shook his head slowly. "I don't think so."

She hadn't thought it possible to hurt any more than she already was. Once again, she'd been wrong. She prayed the dampness on her face was the rain.

"All right." She nodded stiffly, turned. "See you around, then."

"One more thing, Allie."

She wasn't certain she could handle one more thing without crumbling, but she hesitated, glanced over her shoulder. He rose from the bench and closed the short distance between them.

"Will you marry me?"

"What?"

"Like I said, some things need to be said in person." He reached for her hand, lifted her fingers to his lips. "We can go out on a few dates first. We never really had a chance to do that before. Please, Allie, just give me that chance."

"Jordan—"

"Let me romance you. Let me tempt you,

seduce you." He brushed his lips over her knuckles. "Let me love you."

She shuddered at his touch, but fear caught hold of her, had her snagging her hand away. "If this is your idea of a joke, so help me—"

"I love you, Alexis. That's no joke." There was an urgency to his voice now. "I loved you eight years ago, but my pride kept me from going after you. I was so certain you'd come back to me, and when you didn't, I was angry."

If he knew how many times she'd almost gone back to him, how many times she'd packed a bag. How many times she'd actually made it to the airport before her own pride turned her back around. And still, she couldn't tell him. Not yet.

"Not signing those annulment papers was my way of hanging on to you, of having the last say." He shoved his hands into his trouser pockets. "Having control. You're right about that. I did want control. I was certain if I let you go out and do all the things you wanted to do, you'd realize you didn't need me."

That had been the problem, she knew. That she'd needed him so much, had loved him so much, it had scared her.

"What's changed?" She looked into his face, felt her bones melting with that need and that love, wanted so badly to lean into him. "Why would now be different for us? I have a home here, you're at Five Corners. And children—"

"When you're ready." He glanced at a woman pushing a stroller across the street, hurrying to get out of the rain. "I won't lie to you, I want kids—yours, ours. But I need you, Allie. More than my next breath. Everything I have means nothing without you, including Five Corners."

"Are you saying you'd live here, in New York?" She shook her head in disbelief.

"That's exactly what I'm saying." He reached for her hand again. "My heart is with you, wherever you are. Wherever you say. Just be my wife. Love me."

"And Five Corners?" she asked, her voice breathless, her chest strumming as the pieces of her heart pulled together and swelled.

"Trey and I are forming a co-op between Stone Ridge Stables and Five Corners and hired a management company to run it. We bring in a couple more ranches, and we'll have the largest in the entire state. I—we—can spend as little or as much time there as we choose."

"You and Trey?" Good Lord. Two of the strongest, most powerful, most obstinate men she'd ever known—partners? It made her head spin.

But she couldn't think about that now. It didn't even matter. All that mattered was Jordan. Standing here, in the rain, telling her that he loved her. Asking—not telling—her to marry him. To be his wife. To have his babies.

And she *did* want his babies, she knew. Soon.

But first, she wanted him. Wanted to pack eight years' worth of love and life into as short a time as possible. She wouldn't regret the years they were apart, she decided. She would simply look forward to the future. Together.

She watched as he pulled his hand out of his pocket, opened his fingers. She was certain her heart stopped when she saw what he held.

Her wedding ring. The one she'd thrown at him eight years ago. He'd kept it. All these years, he'd actually kept it.

"I love you," he whispered. "Marry me."

She stared at the ring, the simple band of gold. Love and hope and need consumed her. Overwhelmed her.

"Allie, for god sakes," he said raggedly. "Say something, please."

She lifted her gaze to his, felt the tears sliding down her cheeks, mixing with the rain.

"It's about time," she murmured, touching her lips to his. "It's about damn time."

* * * * *

Set in darkness beyond the ordinary world.
Passionate tales of life and death.
With characters' lives ruled by laws the
everyday world can't begin to imagine.

n●cturne

It's time to discover the Raintree trilogy...

New York Times bestselling author
LINDA HOWARD
brings you the dramatic first book
RAINTREE: INFERNO

The Ansara Wizards are rising and the
Raintree clan must rejoin the battle against
their foes, testing their powers, relationships
and forcing upon them lives they never
could have imagined before...

Turn the page for a sneak preview
of the captivating first book
in the Raintree trilogy,
RAINTREE: INFERNO by LINDA HOWARD
On sale April 2.

Dante Raintree stood with his arms crossed as he watched the woman on the monitor. The image was in black and white to better show details; color distracted the brain. He focused on her hands, watching every move she made, but what struck him most was how uncommonly *still* she was. She didn't fidget or play with her chips, or look around at the other players. She peeked once at her down card, then didn't touch it again, signaling for another hit by tapping a fingernail on the table. Just because she didn't seem to be paying attention to the other players, though, didn't mean she was as unaware as she seemed.

"What's her name?" Dante asked.

"Lorna Clay," replied his chief of security, Al Rayburn.

"At first I thought she was counting, but she doesn't pay enough attention."

"She's paying attention, all right," Dante murmured. "You just don't see her doing it." A card counter had to remember every card played. Supposedly counting cards was impossible with the number of decks used by the casinos, but there were those rare individuals who could calculate the odds even with multiple decks.

"I thought that, too," said Al. "But look at this piece of tape coming up. Someone she knows comes up to her and speaks, she looks around and starts chatting, completely misses the play of the people to her left—and doesn't look around even when the deal comes back to her, just taps that finger. And damn if she didn't win. Again."

Dante watched the tape, rewound it, watched it again. Then he watched it a third time. There had to be something he was missing, because he couldn't pick out a single giveaway.

"If she's cheating," Al said with something like respect, "she's the best I've ever seen."

"What does your gut say?"

Al scratched the side of his jaw, considering. Finally, he said, "If she isn't cheating, she's the luckiest person walking. She wins. Week in, week out, she wins. Never a huge amount, but I ran the numbers and she's into us for about five grand a week. Hell, boss, on her way out of the casino she'll stop by a slot machine, feed a dollar in and walk away with at least fifty. It's never the same machine, either. I've had her watched, I've had her followed, I've even looked for the same faces in the casino every time she's in here, and I can't find a common denominator."

"Is she here now?"

"She came in about half an hour ago. She's playing blackjack, as usual.

"Bring her to my office," Dante said, making a swift decision. "Don't make a scene."

"Got it," said Al, turning on his heel and leaving the security center.

Dante left, too, going up to his office. His face was calm. Normally he would leave it to

Al to deal with a cheater, but he was curious. How was she doing it? There were a lot of bad cheaters, a few good ones, and every so often one would come along who was the stuff of which legends were made: the cheater who didn't get caught, even when people were alert and the camera was on him—or, in this case, her.

It was possible to simply be lucky, as most people understood luck. Chance could turn a habitual loser into a big-time winner. Casinos, in fact, thrived on that hope. But luck itself wasn't habitual, and he knew that what passed for luck was often something else: cheating. And there was the other kind of luck, the kind he himself possessed, but it depended not on chance but on who and what he was. He knew it was an innate power and not Dame Fortune's erratic smile. Since power like his was rare, the odds made it likely the woman he'd been watching was merely a very clever cheat.

Her skill could provide her with a very good living, he thought, doing some swift calculations in his head. Five grand a week equaled $260,000 a year, and that was just from his casino. She probably hit them all, careful to keep the numbers relatively low so she stayed under the radar.

He wondered how long she'd been taking him, how long she'd been winning a little here, a little there, before Al noticed.

The curtains were open on the wall-to-wall window in his office, giving the impression, when one first opened the door, of stepping out onto a covered balcony. The glazed window faced west, so he could catch the sunsets. The sun was low now, the sky painted in purple and gold. At his home in the mountains, most of the windows faced east, affording him views of the sunrise. Something in him needed both the greeting and the goodbye of the sun. He'd always been drawn to sunlight, maybe because fire was his element to call, to control.

He checked his internal time: four minutes until sundown. Without checking the sunrise tables every day, he knew exactly when the sun would slide behind the mountains. He didn't own an alarm clock. He didn't need one. He was so acutely attuned to the sun's position that he had only to check within

himself to know the time. As for waking at a
particular time, he was one of those people
who could tell himself to wake at a certain
time, and he did. That talent had nothing to do
with being Raintree, so he didn't have to hide
it; a lot of perfectly ordinary people had the
same ability.

He had other talents and abilities, however,
that did require careful shielding. The long
days of summer instilled in him an almost
sexual high, when he could feel contained
power buzzing just beneath his skin. He had
to be doubly careful not to cause candles to
leap into flame just by his presence, or to start
wildfires with a glance in the dry-as-tinder
brush. He loved Reno; he didn't want to burn
it down. He just felt so damn *alive* with all the
sunshine pouring down that he wanted to let
the energy pour through him instead of
holding it inside.

This must be how his brother Gideon felt
while pulling lightning, all that hot power
searing through his muscles, his veins. They
had this in common, the connection with raw
power. All the members of the far-flung
Raintree clan had some power, some height-

ened ability, but only members of the royal family could channel and control the earth's natural energies.

Dante wasn't just of the royal family, he was the Dranir, the leader of the entire clan. "Dranir" was synonymous with king, but the position he held wasn't ceremonial, it was one of sheer power. He was the oldest son of the previous Dranir, but he would have been passed over for the position if he hadn't also inherited the power to hold it.

Behind him came Al's distinctive knock on the door. The outer office was empty, Dante's secretary having gone home hours before. "Come in," he called, not turning from his view of the sunset.

The door opened, and Al said, "Mr. Raintree, this is Lorna Clay."

Dante turned and looked at the woman, all his senses on alert. The first thing he noticed was the vibrant color of her hair, a rich, dark red that encompassed a multitude of shades from copper to burgundy. The warm amber light danced along the iridescent strands, and he felt a hard tug of sheer lust in his gut. Looking at her hair was almost like looking at fire, and he had the same reaction.

The second thing he noticed was that she was spitting mad.

Silhouette

nocturne™

IT'S TIME TO DISCOVER
THE RAINTREE TRILOGY...

There have always been those among us
who are more than human...

Don't miss the dramatic first book by
New York Times bestselling author

LINDA
HOWARD
RAINTREE:
Inferno

On sale May.

Raintree: Haunted by Linda Winstead Jones
Available June.

Raintree: Sanctuary by Beverly Barton
Available July.

SNLHIBC

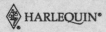

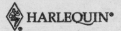

HARLEQUIN®

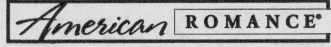

A THREE-BOOK SERIES BY BELOVED AUTHOR

Judy Christenberry

Dallas Duets

What's behind the doors of
the Yellow Rose Lane apartments?
Love, Texas-style!

THE MARRYING KIND
May 2007

Jonathan Davis was many things—a millionaire,
a player, a catch. But he'd never be a husband.
For him, "marriage" equaled "mistake." Diane Black
was a forever kind of woman, a babies-and-minivan
kind of woman. But John was confident he could
date her and still avoid that trap.
Until he kissed her…

Also watch for:
DADDY NEXT DOOR
January 2007

MOMMY FOR A MINUTE
August 2007

Available wherever Harlequin books are sold.

REQUEST YOUR FREE BOOKS!

2 FREE NOVELS PLUS 2 FREE GIFTS!

Silhouette®

Desire®

Passionate, Powerful, Provocative!

YES! Please send me 2 FREE Silhouette Desire® novels and my 2 FREE gifts. After receiving them, if I don't wish to receive any more books, I can return the shipping statement marked "cancel." If I don't cancel, I will receive 6 brand-new novels every month and be billed just $3.80 per book in the U.S., or $4.47 per book in Canada, plus 25¢ shipping and handling per book and applicable taxes, if any*. That's a savings of almost 15% off the cover price! I understand that accepting the 2 free books and gifts places me under no obligation to buy anything. I can always return a shipment and cancel at any time. Even if I never buy another book from Silhouette, the two free books and gifts are mine to keep forever.

225 SDN EEXJ   326 SDN EEXU

Name	(PLEASE PRINT)
Address	Apt.
City	State/Prov. Zip/Postal Code

Signature (if under 18, a parent or guardian must sign)

Mail to the **Silhouette Reader Service™:**
IN U.S.A.: P.O. Box 1867, Buffalo, NY 14240-1867
IN CANADA: P.O. Box 609, Fort Erie, Ontario L2A 5X3

Not valid to current Silhouette Desire subscribers.

Want to try two free books from another line?
Call 1-800-873-8635 or visit www.morefreebooks.com.

* Terms and prices subject to change without notice. NY residents add applicable sales tax. Canadian residents will be charged applicable provincial taxes and GST. This offer is limited to one order per household. All orders subject to approval. Credit or debit balances in a customer's account(s) may be offset by any other outstanding balance owed by or to the customer. Please allow 4 to 6 weeks for delivery.

Your Privacy: Silhouette is committed to protecting your privacy. Our Privacy Policy is available online at www.eHarlequin.com or upon request from the Reader Service. From time to time we make our lists of customers available to reputable firms who may have a product or service of interest to you. If you would prefer we not share your name and address, please check here. ☐

SDES07

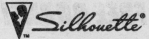

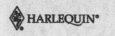